WIDOW DECLARES WAR ON HOLLINGSWORTHS!

Mrs. Pearl Sinclair, 79, told the *Sunrise Gazette* this week that Hollingsworths is trying to pressure her into selling her home and her land to them. "It's a disgrace!" she told the *Gazette*. "A scandal! I don't want to sell.... Hollingsworths say they need it for the parking lot of their new shopping center and cinema complex. That it's the only suitable site. But I say that's rubbish.

"You can tell Amber Hollingsworth from me that I won't be emotionally blackmailed into selling, either. I see now what she was trying to do when she sat here in my kitchen and drank my tea and pretended to be nice to me.... If Amber Hollingsworth comes here again, trying to con me with her sweet smiles and her pretty ways, I'll set my dog on her!"

MIRANDA LEE is Australian, living near Sydney. Born and raised in the bush, she was boarding-school educated and briefly pursued a classical music career before moving to Sydney and embracing the world of computers. Happily married, with three daughters, she began writing when family commitments kept her at home. She likes to create stories that are believable, modern, fast-paced and sexy. Her interests include reading meaty sagas, doing word puzzles, gambling and going to the movies.

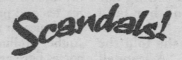

Look out next month for the last title in this breathtaking series:

Scandalous Bride by Diana Hamilton, #1936.

What did Nathan know about his new bride? Theirs had been a whirlwind wedding. Now he was certain she was having an affair with her boss! Their marriage was heading for the rocks, unless Nathan could discover the truth about his scandalous bride....

MIRANDA LEE

Red-Hot and Reckless

Harlequin Books

TORONTO • NEW YORK • LONDON
AMSTERDAM • PARIS • SYDNEY • HAMBURG
STOCKHOLM • ATHENS • TOKYO • MILAN
MADRID • WARSAW • BUDAPEST • AUCKLAND

ISBN 0-373-11930-5

RED-HOT AND RECKLESS

First North American Publication 1998.

Printed in U.S.A.

CHAPTER ONE

AMBER was preoccupied as she inserted the key in the front door. She was thinking of business, as was often the case these days. Amazing, really, how much she was enjoying running the family company. More amazing was the fact that she was pretty good at it.

Okay, so she hadn't quite filled her father's shoes as yet, but their accountant had commented only today that Hollingsworths was looking healthier than ever.

When Amber turned the key and pushed open the front door, she didn't notice her stepmother standing there in the foyer, waiting for her.

'Lord, Beverly!' Amber exclaimed, once she did. 'You gave me a fright. I didn't see you there.'

'Your father wants to see you,' her stepmother announced, her tone terse. 'Straight away.'

'What about?' Amber asked.

'I have no idea.' Beverly stared at her with cold eyes, blinked once, very slowly, then turned, just as slowly, and walked off.

Amber barely resisted pulling a face. Instead, she smothered a sigh and strode across the spacious foyer and down the wide hallway which bisected the right wing of the house, stopping at the first door on the right.

The room inside had once been her father's study, an impressive and very masculine room which had suited its owner and occupier. Twelve months ago, after her father's stroke, it had been converted into a bedroom with a private bathroom. The room opposite the study, once a billiard room, had also been converted—into quarters for her father's live-in male nurse-cum-companion-cum-physio.

Amber's knock was hesitant. Not so the 'come in' which roared through the door. Surprisingly, her father's stroke hadn't affected his speech, or his deep, loud voice. Just occasionally Amber wasn't sure if she thought this fortunate or not.

Gathering herself, she opened the door and walked in.

'Hi, there, Dad,' she said breezily. 'You wanted to see me?'

Dear heaven, would she never get used to seeing his once strong, tanned face looking so gaunt and pale? Or the wheelchair at the foot of the bed? Or that thin, withered leg which Bill was at that moment massaging quite vigorously?

'Hi, there, Bill.' She directed her words towards her father's minder. Bill was a big, bald, plain man in his late thirties. He had a placid nature, which was just as well. 'How's the patient?' Amber asked him. 'He's sounding a bit grumpy.'

'The patient's spitting chips, girlie,' her father jumped in, while Bill merely shrugged and continued the massage. 'So don't try talking around me. It won't work. Leave it, Bill,' he said irritably, and yanked his near-dead limb away from Bill's hold. It dropped onto the bed with a hollow-sounding thud. 'Go and get yourself a drink or something. I have serious business to discuss with Sunrise Point's Businesswoman-of-the-Year, here.'

Bill shrugged again and left the room. He was used to his patient's irascibility. Edward Hollingsworth was not the sort of man to take meekly to inactivity. He was a mover and a shaker. A doer, even at sixty-two years old. Being partially paralysed and lying round in bed most of his day did little for his temper.

'I take it you haven't seen this week's local paper?' Edward Hollingsworth snarled, and leant over to snatch up the newspaper from where it was lying on the pillow next to him. 'I dare say you haven't, or you wouldn't have been looking so pleased with yourself as you came in. Bill always gets me the first copy hot off the press, but shortly all the people in Sunrise will be taking their copies out of their postboxes and learning over their evening meals that Edward Hollingsworth is a ruthless, greedy bastard, and that his daughter is a chip off the old block!'

'What?' Amber gasped.

'Here, read it yourself!' he growled, and shoved the paper forward. She took it and sank down on the side of the huge bed. The headlines brought another gasp to her lips: 'WIDOW DECLARES WAR ON HOLLINGSWORTHS!' And then in smaller print...

Mrs Pearl Sinclair, 79, of Sinclair Farm, Potts Road, told the *Sunrise Gazette* this week that Hollingsworths is trying to pressure her into selling her home and her land to them. 'It's a disgrace!' she told the *Gazette*. 'A scandal! I don't want to sell. I'm a war widow. I came to live here as a new bride nearly sixty years ago. I had my son and daughter here. All my memories are here. This is my home. How can you put a price on memories? Or a home? Hollingsworths say they need it for the car park of their new shopping centre and cinema complex. That it's the only suitable site. But I say that's rubbish. Edward Hollingsworth owns half the coast around here. Let him build his shopping centre somewhere else. I am not going to be bullied into selling him my home!

'And as far as that daughter of his is concerned— you can tell Amber Hollingsworth from me that I won't be emotionally blackmailed into selling, either. I see now what she was trying to do when she came to my house the other day and sat here in my kitchen and drank my tea and pretended to be nice to me. She was just trying to soft-soap me, giving me all that rubbish about wanting to do good for the town. When did any Hollingsworth ever do good for this town? Edward Hollingsworth only ever cared about doing good for himself. I can't see any daughter of his being any better!

'I dare say they'll offer me even more money now. But they can offer me the world and my answer will be the same. No! A resounding no! You tell the Hollingsworth family that from me. And if Amber Hollingsworth comes here again, trying to con me with her sweet smiles and pretty ways, I'll set my dog onto her! I'll have you know that Rocky here was banned from racing because he was a fighter, and he's a very vicious watchdog!'

The article was accompanied by a photograph of the old lady, looking defiant, standing on the front verandah of that wretched house of hers with a decidedly overweight greyhound standing guard by her side.

Amber couldn't help it. She laughed. 'Set the dog onto me? That dog almost loved me to death the day I visited!'

'Amber, this is not a laughing matter,' her father snapped. 'You told me on Monday night that that sale was in the bag. Now, just forty-eight hours later, we have *that* to contend with! You and I both know there *is* no other site for that car park, because there is no other site large enough and flat enough for the complex. You can't build shopping malls on the sides of mountains. And you can't build them too far out of town or you defeat the purpose. We either get the Sinclair farm or this project of yours dies a natural death.'

Amber knew her father was right. Sunrise Point couldn't expand at will, like so many other coastal towns on the north coast of New South Wales, because of logistical reasons. Firstly, no homes or hotels could be built anywhere on the actual point, or right alongside the two accompanying beaches—a national park occupied the foreshores. Secondly, the Great Dividing Range kinked towards the coastline at that point, so that there simply wasn't all that much room for development. As it was, most of the houses were built on slopes.

'Look, I don't know what that devious old lady is up to, Dad,' Amber said, sighing, 'but she couldn't have been nicer or more agreeable on Monday. She said she thought my offer very generous, but just wanted a few days to think it over. She asked me to come back the following Monday. I got the impression the wait was just a formality, that she would sign on the dotted line.'

'Well, something obviously happened during those few days to change her mind. Maybe she talked to someone in her family, and that someone convinced her your offer wasn't generous enough. Call me a cynical old bastard, but I reckon that article there is a ploy to get more money!' And he jabbed his finger at the newspaper.

Amber's stomach tightened. 'You could be right, Dad. And I think I know who that someone is, too. Ben Sinclair. Her grandson. I wouldn't put it past him to want to milk Hollingsworths for every cent he can get.'

'You sound like you know him pretty well, but I have no recollection of a grandson at all!'

'Oh, Dad, surely you remember Ben?' Amber asked irritably. 'He was in my class at school. He came to live here with his grandmother when he was about sixteen. You *must* remember him. He shocked everyone by getting the best exam results of all of us. His tertiary score was in the top two percent of the state. They put his photo in this very paper.'

'What did he look like?'

'Oh, dark hair and eyes. Quite good-looking, really, if you could overlook his permanently sulky expression.'

'Nope. Can't remember him at all. The only boy I remember from your class is Chris Johnson. Whom you would have done well to marry instead of that American playboy you latched onto when I was fool enough to give you an overseas trip as a graduation present.'

'Yes, well, I was too young to marry anyone at that stage. I was only nineteen, you know. I wish you'd stopped me.'

Her father laughed. 'That's like trying to stop the rain falling on a rainforest. You're as stubborn as me once you set your sights on something. No one could have stopped you marrying Chad. At least you had the good sense to divorce him in the end. Pity you took so long about it.

'But back to the issue at hand. What are you going to do about this Sinclair business? I know how you've got your heart set on this complex, daughter, but is it worth a scandal? I've come to like having this town's respect, even if it has been a long time coming. When I get better I'm going to run for Mayor.'

'Then I suggest we do everything possible to get this project up and running. This town *needs* this complex, Dad.'

'I agree, but to build it Hollingsworths needs the Sinclair farm. How do you aim to get it? By offering the old lady more money, like she said?'

'I guess so.'

'And how much money do you think that will entail?'

'I'm not sure...'

Frankly, Amber wasn't sure about anything at that moment. This startling new development had thrown her for a loop. Pearl Sinclair had not seemed all that interested in money the other day. Neither had she seemed the type to bow to pressure, not even Ben's. She was as tough as teak.

Maybe she *was* attached to the ramshackle dump she lived in, Amber mused, but it was hard to imagine so. The house was falling around her ears, and the farm part had long deteriorated into nothing but a chicken coop and a dilapidated barn. The land had also recently had a one-in-twenty-five-year flood rating stamped on the council charts, so on the open market it wasn't worth much.

'Maybe we're reading this all wrong,' Amber speculated. 'Maybe old Pearl just couldn't face the move at her age. Or the search for somewhere else to live. Maybe it was all too daunting.'

'My dear Amber,' came her father's exasperated reply, 'that would not explain her vitriolic and quite personal attack on us. No, this grandson of hers has got in her ear and stirred her all up.'

Her father fell thoughtfully silent. Amber tried to keep her mind empty of thoughts she didn't want to think, and memories she didn't want to remember.

'What about the son and daughter she mentioned?' her father asked abruptly. 'Where are they?'

Amber shrugged. 'I don't know. Either she's estranged from them, or they're dead. I think Ben is her only close relative. Or the only one who visits. And he doesn't visit all that often any more. She was complaining over that cup of tea I had with her that he didn't even come home last Christmas. He lives down in Sydney now, and went off with some new girl-friend. She was pretty upset about it.'

'I see. Well, my guess is the dear boy will be home soon. With bells on. What does he do, do you know?'

'He's a lawyer. Works for some big Sydney law firm.'

'Dear God, that's all we need—having to contend with some clever-boots city lawyer. No doubt he's sniffed a huge profit to be made in all this.'

'He's probably sniffed more than that,' Amber muttered.

Her father's sharp blue eyes narrowed on her. 'What the hell does that mean? Was there ever something between you and this Ben Sinclair? Tell me the truth, daughter. Don't lie. You're a terrible liar, any-way.'

No, I'm not, she thought. I'm a very good liar. I lived a lie all during my six-year marriage to Chad. No one knew how wretched I was. Or what a failure I felt.

'No.' She lied again. 'There was nothing personal between Ben and myself. But he was dirt-poor back then, and as antisocial as you could get. I think he disliked me merely because I was rich.'

'When he reads this article in the paper, he'll dis-like you even more.'

'Maybe he won't read it.'

'Pigs. He's responsible for it, I'll warrant. We can expect Ben Sinclair on our doorstep any day now.'

'How delightful,' she said drily.

Her father's eyes narrowed on her further. 'There's certainly no love lost between you two, is there?'

'Oh, I wouldn't go so far as to say that. We've hardly spoken two words to each other in the past ten years. But he was a nasty piece of goods at school, and I see no reason to believe he's changed. I would imagine that as a man he's just as disagreeable.'

Amber had actually run into him several times dur-ing the three years since her return home. A couple of times in the main street but mostly in church, at Easter and Christmas. Not this last Christmas, how-ever.

She'd known, before his grandmother had told her, that Ben hadn't come home last Christmas. She'd looked for him at the church service. And missed him, she realised all of a sudden. Perverse, when on each previous occasion he'd reduced their encounters to nothing but a distantly cool nod, or a chillingly polite, 'Hello, Amber.'

'Disagreeable or not,' her father snapped, 'you'll have to deal with him if you want to build that complex.'

'We'll see, Dad,' she said, trying not to sound as rattled as she was suddenly feeling. 'We'll see.'

'I have a feeling there's more to this than meets the eye. Watch it, daughter. The last thing I want to see is our family name splashed across next week's headlines in another souped-up scandal!'

CHAPTER TWO

BEN scooped up this week's copy of the *Sunrise Gazette* from the floor then kicked the front door shut behind him. He stripped off the wrapping, tossed the rolled paper onto his favourite armchair for later perusal, then strode out into the kitchen to stuff the shrivelled ball of plastic into the bin.

He grimaced as he reached for the whisky bottle which was sitting in readiness on the starkly white kitchen counter. His other hand up-ended the clean glass which sat next to it. Unscrewing the cap on the bottle, he poured himself a well needed measure.

What a day! What a life! Wall to wall bulldust!

He loosened his blue silk tie with a frustrated yank then retrieved a tray of ice from the fridge, plopping several cubes into the straight Scotch. He was scowling as he snatched up the glass.

Strange. He had always thought being a big-city lawyer would make him supremely happy. He'd have money and kudos. People would look up to him and think he was someone. Women would fall at his feet.

Well, he certainly had money. Corporate law paid very well. How else could he have afforded this snazzy unit overlooking Sydney Harbour? Or the sleek black Saab 9000 CD Turbo which occupied one of his two private car spaces in the underground car park, twenty storeys down?

He gulped down a large swallow of liquid tranquilliser, then frowned at his need for it.

A top-flight legal eagle earned more than most doctors these days, and Ben's six-figure salary satisfied his craving for monetary success. But he hadn't been basking in too much community admiration lately.

The status of lawyers worldwide had slipped somewhat in the past ten years. In a recent poll, public opinion had had them just above politicians and used-car salesmen. People generally thought of lawyers as shysters and rogues who charged exorbitant fees for services which were often ineffectual and inefficient.

The law firm where Ben worked as a junior partner was actually very effective *and* efficient, but very, very expensive. The rate per hour for a consultancy alone was exorbitant. Once a client actually hired them, the costs began to soar. Certainly they got results, which perhaps justified the high fees. Ben appreciated the adage that you only got what you paid for. It was the petty but hidden charges which rankled.

When he'd noticed yesterday that they'd started billing clients two dollars for every miserable photocopy, he'd seen red. But when he'd pointed out this questionable charge to one of the senior partners this afternoon, he'd been told curtly and coldly that crusading lawyers worked for Legal Aid, not one of the largest and most successful law firms in Sydney.

'Maybe working for Legal Aid might not be such

a bad idea,' Ben muttered into his drink, feeling quite dissatisfied with his professional life at that moment.

Admittedly, he could not complain over his private life and his score rate with the opposite sex. There were an incredible number of beautiful women in Sydney who obviously weren't as discriminating as the public over where or how you earned your money, as long as you drove a great car, dressed in even greater suits and took them to the greatest restaurants.

Over the past few years Ben had dated a steady succession of society beauties and career colleagues, plus the odd sprinkling of unashamedly ambitious gold-diggers. In a weird kind of way he rather preferred these last steely-hearted souls, because he empathised with what drove them to be so accommodating.

Poverty.

Or an aversion to it.

Ben knew about being poor. And he didn't plan on being poor ever again. Or being without a pretty woman on his arm. It was just a pity his choice of profession hadn't won him the personal esteem and respect he coveted as well.

'Still,' he muttered as he lifted the straight Scotch to his lips once more, 'two out of three ain't bad. Stop griping, Ben. Would you rather still be living with Gran back at Sunrise Point? Every time you become disgruntled with your life, think about the life you once had—living with a crotchety old lady on a ramshackle farm, being treated by everyone in town—and at school—as an outsider. And, worst of all, being looked down upon by the one girl you so desperately wanted.'

Amber Hollingsworth...

Ben's top lip curled as he thought of her—as he still did far too often. What an insufferably spoiled, self-centred little snob she'd been!

But so bloody beautiful. The type of girl boys like him could only dream about. Blonde, of course. With hair down to her waist, legs up to her armpits and perfect, perky breasts which had jiggled tauntingly as she walked along.

And what a walk that had been! A cross between a wanton wiggle and an arrogant strut. That prettily pert nose always up in the air, her slender shoulders well back, her spine straight, but her hips swaying seductively from side to side as those long legs propelled her along.

There hadn't been a boy in school—or a man in town—who hadn't stopped to watch Amber Hollingsworth walk by.

Except me, Ben recalled, with the beginnings of a rueful smile.

Oh, he'd watched. But surreptitiously. Sneakily.

He'd never stopped and gawked. He would never have given the bitch the satisfaction.

And she *had* been a bitch. To him. But only to him.

To all the other boys at school, butter wouldn't have melted in her mouth. She'd been so sweet to them, flashing that megawatt smile of hers, widening those falsely innocent big blue eyes and fluttering those impossibly long, curling eyelashes.

All *he'd* got from the first day his gran dropped him off at school, the day after his sixteenth birthday, had been pitying glances, soon followed by scornful comments.

'Really, Ben. Don't you own any other clothes?'

'Really, Ben. I don't know how they do things down in the city, but up here we wear deodorant.'

'Really, Ben. Didn't your mother teach you it's rude to stare?'

He scowled as he thought of that one time she'd caught him doing just that. Staring at her.

It had been a year or so after the welfare department had sent him to live with his gran. On that particular summer's day Amber had been lying on the grass under a tree in the school grounds during the lunch-hour. It had been very hot, and she'd undone the top two buttons of her white school blouse. From where Ben had been sitting on a nearby bench he'd been able to see all of her cleavage and most of one of those perfect breasts, inadequately encased in expensive white lace.

Ben had been pretty sure she'd known he was ogling her all along, and had even shifted her body slightly to give him a better view. Finally, when he'd been totally engrossed in drooling over those luscious curves, her head had snapped round to catch him in the act. He hadn't looked away, as he might usually have done. He'd just kept on staring.

For a split second he could have sworn she'd blushed—although it might have been the thirty-five degrees centigrade warming her cheeks—but then she'd tossed her hair back, lifted her nose and delivered that scathing reproach about his mother and his rude staring.

Ben had hated her from that moment. Hated her and wanted her at the same time. He'd vowed to get even with the high and mighty Miss Amber Hollingsworth if it was the last thing he did.

His need for revenge, however, had not been as great as the other, far more basic need she'd evoked in him—as had been demonstrated the night of their graduation ball.

He hadn't taken a partner. Not because he couldn't find one, but because if he couldn't take Amber Hollingsworth, he wouldn't take anyone. Such had been his obsession with her.

Actually, there had been several girls in class who would have happily been his partner—not to mention his latest girlfriend. By then, at nearly nineteen, Ben's tall, lean frame had filled out nicely, and some of his female classmates had suddenly seemed to find his looks quite sexy.

Ben had cut his sexual teeth on their unexpected and quite brazen willingness during his last two terms in high school. But none had held his interest beyond a couple of encounters. For one thing he hadn't had enough money to date a steady girlfriend. For another he'd quickly grown to despise their easiness.

Despite her overt sensuality and nymph-like beauty, Amber Hollingsworth had still been a virgin. Everyone in school had known that. If she hadn't been, her latest boyfriend would have shouted his success to the rooftops and beyond.

Chris Johnson had thought he was God's gift to girls, with his sun-streaked blond hair and bronzed torso. Sunrise High's best surfer had reputedly made out with every half-decent-looking bird in school, and had set his sights on the prize of prizes—the beautiful blonde daughter of the richest man in town.

So far, without much success, it had seemed.

Ben had set out to look as good as he could that night. It had been a matter of pride, not hope.

He'd saved every cent for weeks from what he'd earned selling free-range eggs door to door after school, and had hired a proper formal outfit. A smart black tux, a dazzling white shirt and a crisp black bow-tie. He'd even bought new black shoes. He'd also had his unruly black waves professionally trimmed. Gran had pronounced him very handsome indeed as she drove him to the school hall in her rusty old pick-up truck.

Amber had looked more beautiful that night than he'd ever seen her. Her dress had been virginal white, yet very sexy. Just down to her knees, with a floaty skirt and a tight top with tiny straps over her shoulders.

Ben hadn't been able to take his eyes off her. He hadn't bothered to hide his feelings this time, letting his crazed but usually controlled desire off the leash for once, gobbling her up with a hungry gaze which no girl could have mistaken.

She hadn't mistaken it. And she'd looked back. Long, agitated glances which had carried an intriguingly fearful quality, as though she hadn't wanted to look back at him, but couldn't help herself.

Her reluctant but compelling interest had stirred a wildly reckless confidence in Ben. When her boyfriend had abandoned Amber to go to the men's room around midnight, Ben had sauntered across the dance floor towards her.

'Come for a walk with me,' he said, his words not a polite request but a blunt order. He often adopted an arrogant attitude with girls these days, and, perversely, it seemed to work. But he'd never dreamt he would talk to Amber Hollingsworth in such an offhanded fashion. Usually just her presence could deflate his confidence, though not a certain part of his anatomy. At this very moment, every single part of him was raging with a wild desire.

Her lovely blue eyes widened. She might have tossed her hair, but it was up, with long tantalising tendrils curling around her beautiful face.

'Who do you think you're talking to, Ben Sinclair?' she retorted, though shakily. 'I'm not one of those little sluts you've been running around with who let you do what you like down behind the gym.'

'Just shut up and do as you're told,' he muttered, and, taking her hand, curled his fingers forcefully through hers. An electric charge raced down his arm—and up hers, judging by the look on her face.

'Come on,' he insisted, and began pulling her through the throng of gyrating dancers. Several of their graduating classmates stared after them.

Ben suspected he might have Chris Johnson to contend with the following day, but he didn't care. At that moment Amber was meekly following his lead, and looking just a little bewildered by her own submissive behaviour. Ben was quite blown away by the dizzying feeling of power charging along his already dangerously heated bloodstream.

He didn't take her behind the gym. He took her down behind the staff block, which was further away. It was also darker. He drew her into a recessed doorway and pressed her up against the smooth wooden door. He could hardly see her face in the darkness, but he could smell her heady perfume and feel her trembling body.

He didn't say a word. He just started kissing her. And touching her. All over.

She didn't stop him. In fact she was soon actively aiding and abetting him. Kissing him back, touching him back. She couldn't seem to get enough of him.

His own fierce arousal quickly transformed to a passionate resolve. He would be her first. He would show her how much she meant to him, how much he'd always wanted her.

And ten minutes later he was doing just that, doing it while they stood there in that darkened doorway, doing it with a startling and shocking ease. She clung to his shoulders and whispered his name as he surged deeply—and unimpeded—into her.

There was no protest or cry of pain from his supposedly virginal victim, only a low moan of the most ecstatic pleasure. She began moving on him with an amazingly practised skill, squeezing and releasing his flesh as no girl had ever done to him before.

Stunned and stupidly distressed, he'd immediately withdrawn, standing there in a speechless state as he tried to come to terms with his shock. Her only reaction was a dazed groan of disappointment at having her satisfaction snatched away from her at the last moment.

His own far more crippling disappointment suddenly found voice in his tongue, and he tore strips off her in words which he could not remember afterwards. He only knew he called her all sorts of names. He didn't mean most of them, of course. It was his hurt talking. He'd been a fool to put her on such a pedestal.

But she had the last word anyway. She put the seal on what he meant to her and how she really felt about him...by not saying anything. By turning up her nose and simply going back to the ball and dancing with Chris as if nothing had happened. She looked right through him when he came back inside. When he kept staring at her, she laughed, then curled her arms much more tightly around Chris' neck.

He'd been shocked. And shattered. He'd never

known a girl could be like that. Ruthless. Unfeeling. Cruel. He had heard that laugh in his head for years, repeatedly imagining how that evening had ended for her, wrapped naked in Chris's arms, giving him all she'd given Ben. But much, much more.

Ben shuddered at his masochistic thoughts, forcibly snapping his mind back to the present. He hadn't thought about Amber Hollingsworth in such depth for a long time. God knew why she still haunted him. She wasn't worth thinking about. Females like her were only good for one thing.

Ben strode back into his living room, and there, waiting for him, was his hometown paper, the one which kept him in touch—not only with Sunrise, but with Miss High-and-Mighty herself. It had told him about her marriage to an American playboy all those years ago. It had informed him of her divorce and return home three years back.

Ben had hoped her homecoming after her divorce was only a temporary thing, but when her father had had a stroke early last year Ben had been shocked to read in the paper that Amber had taken the helm of Hollingsworths—a most unlikely event, considering she had never been academically minded. At school she'd been more interested in her hair and her nails than in computers or business studies.

But clearly she'd found her feet being a minor tycoon, and she meant to stay. A week before Christmas he'd read in the *Gazette* about her grand plans for a shopping and cinema complex for the area.

Her ongoing presence in town was one of the reasons Ben had avoided going home last Christmas. His gran always dragged him along to church, and the thought of running into Amber there, as he seemed to every Christmas, had been enough to make him accept Brenda's invitation to spend the Christmas break with her and her family.

A mistake, as it had turned out. Even putting up with another disturbing encounter with Amber would have been preferable to enduring four days with Brenda's incredibly snooty family. They made the Hollingsworths look poor by comparison. And almost normal. Seeing the real Brenda in action—my God, she actually called her parents Mumsy and Daddykins!—had dampened his ardour for her in bed, and he hadn't taken her out since.

Why was it, Ben wondered, that he knew nothing would ever dampen his ardour for Amber Hollingsworth? She could be as bitchy as she liked. As snobbish. As promiscuous. As ambitious. Anything, really. And he would still want her.

Ben glared down at the rolled up paper. He conceded that it was this ongoing obsession with Amber Hollingsworth which made him keep on subscribing to this pathetic rag. Why couldn't he get over his masochistic fascination with the female? Why couldn't he bear to sever the link once and for all by cancelling his subscription and never returning to Sunrise Point, not even at Christmas?

It seemed that such a final action was beyond him.

For one thing he could not hurt his gran by never returning to the farm. She was a right pain in the neck, but she had been good to him when he'd desperately needed someone. If it hadn't been for his gran's support and encouragement, he probably would have ended up on the other side of the law.

Ben accepted that this coming Easter—which was less than a month away—he would drive back to Sunrise Point and sit in that damned church again, dreading yet aching to see his eternal torment one more time.

He drained the last of his drink, placed the empty glass on the coffee table, scooped up the paper from his armchair and plonked himself down. With angry sweeping movements, he spread the paper out on his lap.

The headline jumped out at him, and then the photo of his gran. His heart began to thump as he read the story, a mounting fury sending his blood charging hotly around his body. But along with the fury was frustration. Why hadn't his Gran told him? Why hadn't she rung?

He practically ground his teeth as he thought of Amber Hollingsworth, smugly thinking she could sweet-talk a seemingly defenceless old lady into parting with her home and land. For a pittance, no doubt.

Well, she didn't know his gran, did she? Amber thought she could have anything she wanted, when she wanted it, simply because she'd been born rich and beautiful. Her motto in life was, 'I want. And what I want, I get. And when I don't want it any more, I get out'.

He felt sorry for that poor bastard who'd married her. No doubt she'd led him a merry dance. She'd led every male who cared about her merry dances. Chris Johnson had been given short shrift straight after that graduation ball. He'd been no longer wanted once the richest man in town gave his darling daughter a fancy trip around the world. Chris had bad-mouthed Amber around town for months afterwards, finally revealing the true nature of their relationship. His opinion of her was no higher than Ben's own.

Ben clenched his teeth hard in his jaw. He'd denied her instant gratification once, and, by God, he'd make sure she didn't have it this time, too.

No way was Ben going to allow his Gran to sell that land to the Hollingsworths. He'd buy the useless damned farm himself, if need be! The time for getting even with the Princess of Sunrise Point had finally arrived.

CHAPTER THREE

'PERHAPS you don't realise it, Amber, but, aside from that scandalous business in the paper yesterday, your father is very disappointed in you.'

Amber closed her eyes momentarily, grateful that her back was turned to her stepmother. Every time they were alone these days, Beverly trotted out some subtle criticism or other. Plus some not so subtle criticisms lately.

It hadn't always been like that. When Edward Hollingsworth had first started dating Beverly, over ten years ago, she'd been all milk and honey around Amber. Amber had quite liked the woman, despite feeling naturally jealous that her father suddenly had *no* time for her at all. When they'd married, during Amber's last year at school, she'd tried to be happy that her father had finally found someone to share his life with. His first wife, Amber's mother, had tragically drowned only three years after their wedding, and less than two years after Amber's birth.

Beverly had been an attractive widow in her forties back then, with a grown son of her own who didn't live with her. She'd kept up a very convincing sweet stepmamma act even after the marriage, though Amber had always wondered whose idea it had been to send her overseas as soon as she'd left school. And she suspected Beverly had been thrilled when Amber had married an American.

It was easy to be nice from a distance. Over the telephone she'd been sweet as apple pie. But when Amber had come home to live, suddenly she could do nothing right in her stepmother's eyes. Yet Amber had tried to stay out of her way, going every day to the office with her father and leaving the home front totally in her stepmother's hands.

Beverly's change in attitude had become even more marked, however, after her husband's stroke. Clearly she had hoped that her own son, Carl—who had a business and marketing degree—would be brought up from Sydney and put in charge of the family company, which had a wide range of business interests. Hollingsworths Pty Ltd owned several shops in town, as well as all over northern New South Wales. They also had investments in holiday resorts, units, restaurants, and a lot of land.

When Edward had given the job as acting managing director to Amber, Beverly had been hard pushed to hide her resentment. When Amber had begun making a success of her new position, the gloves had really come off.

Beverly especially hated the new adult closeness which had developed between father and daughter. She was always trying to drive wedges between them. The article in the paper had provided her with a wonderful weapon over the past twenty-four hours. But it seemed it wasn't enough.

Amber finished pouring herself a glass of white wine whilst pondering her amazing capacity for making enemies over the years. Most of the girls at school had loathed her. Her stepbrother, Carl, despised her. Her ex-husband, Chad, had tried to kill her when she'd said she was leaving him. Chris, her high school sweetheart, had never forgiven her for making a fool of him on that ghastly night.

But all of them paled into insignificance beside what Ben Sinclair felt for her. No doubt murder would be too good for Amber Hollingsworth, in his opinion.

But she wouldn't think about Ben just now. Thinking about Ben always disturbed her far too much, and she needed every ounce of composure she owned to combat Beverly once she got on her 'tear Amber down to size' bandwagon.

She turned to face her stepmother, feeling oddly curious over what the woman had come up with this time. 'Really, Beverly? In what other way is Dad disappointed in me?'

'Just look at you,' Beverly said, with a faint curl of her thinnish upper lip. 'Twenty-eight years old and you're husbandless, childless and sexless.'

Amber's eyebrows shot up. 'Sexless, Beverly? What on earth do you mean?' No point in defending the husbandless and childless part. They were all too evident. And if her stepmother's tactless remark hurt, she certainly wasn't going to show it. Amber was a past master at hiding hurts.

'You know very well what I mean,' Beverly continued curtly. 'Oh, you're beautiful enough, I suppose, though far too thin in my opinion...'

Amber's blue eyes moved tellingly over her stepmother's growing bulk, but she said nothing. She didn't have to. Beverly's snaky remark had said it all.

'You haven't dated once in the three years you've been living at home since your divorce. Clearly you don't care for male company.'

Amber sipped her drink as she walked slowly across the finely furnished lounge room and settled herself on the silk brocade sofa. Beverly was sitting in her usual chair, nursing a generous whisky and soda.

'You're wrong, Beverly,' she said, quite calmly. 'I like male company a lot. I prefer it, actually, to female company. I enjoy talking with Father and the other men I work with very much. As for your accusation about my dating, I've been out to dinner with several men this past year.'

'That's not what I mean and you know it,' Beverly snapped. 'They were just business dinners. One could not call them proper dates by any stretch of the imagination.'

'Oh, I see—you're talking about *sex*!' Amber said bluntly, having learnt since going into business that, occasionally, attack was the best defence.

'That's right. I'm talking about sex. Is that a dirty word with you?'

'Not if it's accompanied by the word 'love', Beverly. I'm one of those peculiar girls who needs to be in love to enjoy making love.'

And that's the most hypocritical thing you've ever said in your life, whispered her conscience. A lie of the most mammoth proportions. A whopper, in fact. The most memorable lovemaking you ever experienced in your life was when love had nothing to do with it.

Amber tried to keep the hot memory of that incredibly brief and incredibly torrid encounter from tumbling into her mind. But it was impossible.

She was back there in her head, and in her body. Behind the staff block, pressed up against the darkened door, panting as Ben pushed her panties aside and entered her as they stood there.

My God, she could still remember how it had felt as he'd done it to her! She'd been consumed by a wild, hot pleasure, plus the most compelling need. How would it have felt if he'd continued? she'd often wondered since.

She hadn't been sure why he'd stopped at first. Till he'd sneered his contempt at her.

'You might be incredibly beautiful,' he'd snarled, 'and you might be filthy rich. But underneath that high and mighty touch-me-not air you're nothing but a slut, Amber Hollingsworth. A cheap little slut! Don't go imagining for one moment I really like you.

I just wanted to show you how easily I could have you. But, quite frankly, I've never been partial to girls who open their legs at the drop of a hat.'

If he'd been expecting her to argue, or cry, or fall apart, he'd been sadly mistaken. Amber had always possessed a fierce self-protective pride which made her react to hurt and embarrassment—and, yes, shame —by withdrawing behind a façade, a shell of cool, even icy indifference.

People often thought her a snob at times like that— or a hard-hearted bitch—but that was not so. It was simply a survival mechanism she'd learnt as a little girl when she hadn't had a mother to advise or protect her. In those days her father had rarely been home, leaving the childminding to paid help who hadn't given a damn about Amber on a personal level. It had been easier to withdraw from a distressful or confusing situation than ask a virtual stranger how to handle it. Eventually it had become an automatic behaviour pattern to deal with any kind of emotional conflict.

Which was why she'd always behaved so badly around Ben Sinclair. From the first moment he'd walked into their class, when she'd been fifteen, she'd been bewildered by her feelings for him. She'd been strangely drawn to those dark, angry eyes and his intriguingly antisocial personality. She hadn't liked him, but she'd been attracted nevertheless. Oh, how she'd wanted him to look at her, to chase after her like most of the other boys in school. When he hadn't, she'd tried to rouse some sort of reaction by making sarcastic remarks.

On the one day she'd caught him actually staring at her, with undisguised lust in that brooding black gaze of his, she'd been in danger of self-combustion. So rattled had she been by the instant heat he'd evoked in her, she'd only just managed to hide her fluster behind another of her highly caustic comments.

There was no doubt she'd hurt him that time with her barb, for he'd glared at her with hatred in his eyes. After that encounter he had not looked at her again with anything other than contempt.

Not till the night of the graduation ball…

Dear heaven, she'd nearly died when he'd walked into the school hall that night. He'd been smoulderingly handsome in that black dinner suit. He'd looked a man where the rest of her classmates had been just boys.

And he'd looked at her as a man would have looked at her.

His very adult desire had seared across the dance floor, sending darts of fire licking along her veins. She hadn't been able to stop glancing back at him; hadn't been able to stop wanting him to ask her to dance. Yet when he'd finally come over, he hadn't asked her to dance. He'd asked her to go outside with him.

She'd known what he wanted. She'd heard the recent rumours about him, how he only took girls outside from school dances for one thing.

Yet she'd gone with him. Not only gone with him,

but let him. Let him kiss her, touch her. Let him do what she had never let Chris do, never let any boy do before.

Not for one moment had she even thought of stopping him. Her body had had a mind of its own. Had been burning for him. Reaching for him. Begging for him. It was only afterwards that she'd realised it hadn't hurt. No pain at all. Only the wildest, sweetest pleasure. Her flesh had opened and closed around his as though it had had a secret agenda, as though this had been what it had been waiting for all its life.

The hurt had come later—when he withdrew, when he spat his appalling contempt at her, when she understood that he'd done what he'd done out of some kind of sick revenge for all those times she'd looked at *him* with seeming contempt.

Naturally she'd had to protect herself from the blinding emotional pain which had threatened to overwhelm her. Dear God, she'd just given her virginity to him. And there he was, calling her a cheap slut!

Spitting back a counter-attack in words would have been not only inadequate but impossible at that moment. So she'd retreated behind her usual hard-nosed shell. She'd managed somehow to return to the dance, to find Chris and pretend she'd just been outside for some fresh air. He hadn't found out the truth till later, when her female classmates had been kind enough to tell him. She'd steeled herself when Ben had walked back inside. She'd even managed to laugh at something Chris had said, and, when she'd looked over

Chris's shoulder at him one last time, Ben's face had been filled with even more contempt than before.

'The only person you have ever loved, Amber Hollingsworth,' her stepmother sniped, snapping Amber back to the present, 'is yourself!'

'You're entitled to your opinion, Beverly,' Amber said coolly. 'But you're wrong. I love my father very much. And he loves me very much.'

'Oh, I know that. Your father is a fool when it comes to his precious darling daughter. He gave you the business to run in the same way he let you trot along to work with him every day. Just to keep you happy. To make up to you for your supposedly miserable marriage and divorce.

'As if you ever loved that Chad person in the first place!' she raved on. 'All he was to you was another sugar-daddy who indulged you as shamelessly as Edward did. But when his money started running out, you left him. If you cared for your father at all,' Beverly scoffed, 'you'd stop playing at being a tycoon and give him what he really wants. A grandchild.'

Amber was taken aback. 'A grandchild!'

'Yes, of course. Men like Edward like to see their line continued. Unfortunately I was too old when we married to give your father more children.'

'Dad has never said anything to me about wanting a grandchild,' Amber said stiffly.

'Neither would he. But I know he would like nothing better than to see you happily married and pregnant. But you and I know that isn't going to come about, don't we, Amber? You were married six years and never had a baby. But there again, having a family wasn't the aim of that marriage, was it? It was money. Too bad there wasn't much left for a decent divorce settlement. And now...now you've got your sights set on other goals. You're into power these days. Power and position.'

Amber could only stand so much. She stood up, her hand tightening around her glass to stop it from shaking. 'Now you look here, Beverly. I'll have you know that—'

The telephone ringing interrupted her counter-attack. Amber knew June, the housekeeper, was busy cooking the dinner, and Bill was giving her father his evening massage, so she strode across the room and out into the hallway, sweeping up the receiver.

'Amber Hollingsworth,' she said, her businesslike tone a reflection of the control she was trying to muster. But her temper was fairly bubbling at Beverly's unjust accusations.

'Hello, Amber,' a cool male voice drawled down the line. 'I'm so glad to find you home.'

'Ben,' she croaked, then swallowed to clear the instant thickening in her throat.

'Right in one. I'm surprised you recognised my voice. Or were you expecting my call?'

'Er...'

He laughed. It was not a warm sound. 'You seem at a loss for words. How unlike you, Amber. I recall you were always very good with your tongue.'

At that moment, Amber's tongue lay uselessly in her mouth. Not so that awful night, she recalled. It had danced with Ben's in an erotic tango during kisses which hadn't been kisses but a total seduction of her senses—and her conscience.

But of course he wasn't referring to that.

'The silent treatment might have worked for you in the past, Amber,' Ben went on coldly, 'but not this time. I've been trying to ring Gran, but she's taken the phone off the hook. Why would that be, I wonder? I can only imagine she's getting calls she doesn't like.

'Whatever, I'll be leaving here first thing in the morning and should be in Sunrise by mid-afternoon. I just thought I'd let you know that if you have any ideas of threatening Gran, or doing anything at all that might be construed as harassment, then I'll have you in court so fast it will make your head spin.'

Amber found her voice at last. 'But I would never do anything like that!'

'Now, why is it I have no confidence in that sweet assurance? Have you spoken to Gran since the paper came out?'

'No.' She'd been going to drive out today, but in the end had decided not to. She'd spent the day going over the plans for the complex and seeing if there was any alternative to putting the car park on Sinclair land. There was. But it was far too expensive. Still, it was a solution of a kind, if her back ended up against the wall. Sunrise was going to get its complex, even if Hollingsworths had to take a loss!

'I'm surprised,' came Ben's droll remark. 'I thought you'd be out there, rolling out some more honey-tongued arguments to change Gran's mind.'

'Believe it or not, Ben Sinclair,' Amber snapped, 'but when I spoke to your grandmother the other day she seemed very agreeable to the idea of selling. And my offer was *very* generous—triple what that land is worth on the open market. I have no idea what changed her mind, or gave her the attitude she expressed in the paper. Unless it was *you*,' she added tartly.

His momentary silence surprised Amber.

'I haven't spoken to Gran since last Sunday night,' he said curtly at last. 'Might I ask when you made this very generous offer?'

'Monday.'

'Well, as you can see, I had nothing to do with Gran's supposed change of attitude. Maybe you mistook her agreement in the first place. I would imagine you're pretty used to assuming most people would do what you want, Amber. The Sinclairs must be proving a bit of a thorn in your side.'

Amber gritted her teeth. 'I don't think I mistook her attitude at all. Look, if you'll be home tomorrow afternoon, I'd like the opportunity to speak to you both together. I believe, once I explain the full situation, you'll be able to make your gran see how important this complex really is to Sunrise Point's future. Ben, you have no idea how many local people don't have jobs. Especially amongst the young.'

'My God, Amber, this new you is quite a stunning change from the old Amber. *She* wouldn't have given a damn about Sunrise Point's future. After all, she couldn't get out of the old hometown fast enough. The Amber I came to know and love certainly wouldn't have sounded so passionate about things local and economical. I'm sure I will find it fascinating to hear your selling spiel.

'Be at the farm at four,' he ordered brusquely. 'But don't bother bringing the Hollingsworth chequebook. Because we're not selling. Not now. Not ever.'

He hung up, leaving Amber in a state of mounting fury. Who did that supercilious, sarcastic bastard think he was? No one had left town more quickly than he had. No one was more selfish—or less socially conscious.

As for his gran, it was *her* land still, wasn't it? If Amber could persuade her to sell, then Ben Sinclair could just butt out.

She wouldn't be at the farm at four. She'd get there at three, with a damned sight more than the Hollingsworth chequebook in hand. She'd have a few other subtle enticements up her sleeve which an old lady might appreciate.

Ben wanted war? Well, he'd get war!

'Who was that?' Beverly demanded to know.

Amber replaced the receiver and turned to face her sour-faced stepmother. Beverly wanted war too, it seemed. Still, there was no point in lying to her.

'Ben Sinclair,' Amber said a touch aggressively. 'Pearl Sinclair's grandson.'

Beverly's eyebrows lifted, then fell. 'Your father said he'd be in touch. What did he want?'

'To see me. Out at the farm. Tomorrow afternoon.'

'So what's he like, this Ben Sinclair?'

'Tall, dark and handsome.'

'Really! How old?'

'Thirtyish,' Amber guessed. He'd been about a year older than herself, and she was twenty-nine next birthday.

'Smart?'

'Super-smart, and sexy as hell.'

Beverly's eyebrows lifted some more. *Really!*

'He's also a bastard of the first order!'

Beverly blinked. 'Goodness, Amber, I've never heard you speak so passionately about a man before. Maybe I was wrong. Maybe you're not sexless after all. Maybe you just need the right male to bring out the fire in you. I'm intrigued. I think I shall invite this Ben Sinclair to dinner.'

'Don't you dare.'

'Amber, this is *my* home. I will invite whom I please.'

'I think Dad might have something to say about that.'

'I think your father will approve wholeheartedly. He always says the best place for one's enemies is under your own roof where you can see them. I'll go ask him.'

She swanned off, leaving Amber to smoulder all by herself.

Oh, go and invite him to dinner, she thought at last with reckless anger. I don't care. At least that way I'll have all *my* current enemies present under the one roof as well!

CHAPTER FOUR

BEN cursed the Pacific Highway all the way home. Dangerous damned road. The government ought to be skinned alive for not spending the money and turning it into a dual highway from Sydney to Brisbane. It was no wonder he didn't visit Gran as often as he should. You took your life in your hands every time you got behind a wheel and headed north along the coast road.

His watch said a quarter to three as he reached the top of Wingaroo Mountain then began the slow, winding descent which would take him down into the valley and the town of Sunrise.

Thank God he would arrive at the farm in plenty of time to be unwound and prepared for Amber's arrival around four. And in plenty of time to have a good chat with Gran. He still hadn't been able to contact her by telephone. Clearly she'd taken it permanently off the hook. He would have something to say about *that* when he got home—*and* her not telling him anything about the Hollingsworths' offer.

Gran was an independent and stubborn old lady. Hadn't she steadfastly refused his offers of money to make her life easier? She wouldn't even let him pay to have the old farmhouse painted. Gran had never asked anybody for anything. And was proud of it!

But there were times when you should ask your family for help.

And he was her only family now. His mum had finally passed away last year, after spending endless years in and out of hospitals, her liver finally giving up the ghost. His uncle Jack, Gran's eldest offspring, had been long gone, a victim of the Vietnam war. Gran had outlived all her own brothers and sisters, and her various nieces and nephews didn't give a damn about their ornery old aunt Pearl.

So there was just him left to stand up for her. And to stop the likes of Amber Hollingsworth from spoiling the old lady's last years. If Gran wanted to *die* on that decrepit old farm, then she had every right to, and that suddenly self-righteous bitch wasn't going to make an old lady feel guilty for clinging to her memories.

Ben could hardly believe the conversation he'd had with Amber last night, or the way she'd trotted out all that bleeding heart stuff about the town's future and unemployment and such. Saint Amber Hollingsworth! Not likely. Next thing she'd be running for Mayor, like her father had several years back.

Everyone in Sunrise knew Edward Hollingsworth had only run for local government to protect his business interests in the area, not because he was a civic-minded soul. That was why he hadn't won the town's vote. Gran was right. You could never trust a

Hollingsworth's motivation, especially when they started spouting forth high-minded philosophies. Ben knew Amber Hollingsworth's priorities. And they began and ended with Amber Hollingsworth! Leopards didn't change their spots.

Ben carefully negotiated the roundabout at the bottom of the hill and headed for the town centre, slowing as he entered the wide but almost empty main street. For a Friday afternoon, it was certainly pretty dead. Only half a dozen cars were parked in the middle.

He slowed further and started to frown. Half the shops were vacant, he noted, with 'For Lease' signs in their bare windows. Groups of young people slouched on the corners and outside the Blue Gum Café, looking dejected. Most were smoking. Some were sitting in the gutters. All the males glared at him driving by as though he had no right to be driving such a great car. The girls just stared.

The thought niggled that Amber might not have exaggerated the unemployment problem in town. Sunrise was looking pretty poorly.

But that didn't mean she had to build her fancy new shopping centre right next to his Gran's farm, Ben argued silently. Surely Hollingsworths could build it somewhere else!

Yeah, like where? came the next niggling thought. Gran's farm was surrounded by the only flat land for miles not already built on.

Ben's lips pressed into a thin line as he accelerated

out through the other side of the main street, swerving round the potholes on the inadequately tarred road which led to his destination.

'Damn and blast,' he muttered, when his front wheel bumped into a hole he didn't see. He would have to get a wheel alignment now, before driving back to Sydney.

His already dark mood deteriorated, and when he rounded the last corner and saw a snazzy little white car parked outside Gran's front gate, and a certain long-legged blonde getting out from behind the wheel —at only three o'clock!—Ben saw red.

He relished the alarm in Amber's big blue eyes as he swung his Saab in alongside her. He didn't think she was worried about his running her down—more likely about being caught arriving suspiciously early for her appointment. She was looking as guilty as hell as he switched off his engine.

Ben climbed out from the air-conditioned comfort of his car into the humid heat of Sunrise in summer, and for a few seconds he just leant on the bonnet of his car and let his eyes drift over her in a deliberately slow appraisal.

Amber had always been worth a slow appraisal, and this time Ben's anger was a good protection from the usual effect her face and figure had on him.

There was no doubt she was a stunning-looking woman, even if at that moment she was dressed like a hokey-pokey country girl in a pink and white polka dot sundress, with her long blonde hair in a girlish plait down her back. He'd rather expected her to show up today in a tailored suit befitting her new executive position. Either black or red. All the businesswomen in Sydney chose red or black for power dressing.

Either Amber wasn't into suits, or she had deliberately chosen to dress as she had today for some specific reason. He had to admit the innocent country look was very fetching. And potentially disarming.

Ben's gaze finally reached her white-sandalled feet and the pink painted toenails peeping through, then worked its way back up her bare, tanned legs, past the shapely calves and nice knees, over the full skirt and nipped in waistline, lingering on the outline of her high, firm breasts which were demurely encased this day, not pushed up together as they had been on that other incredible occasion.

It had annoyed him over the years that not once that night had he actually touched her breasts. Not naked. Yet doing so had been a persistent fantasy both before that night...and since...

Thinking about her breasts naked was his undoing. His flesh gave an involuntary leap and his eyes jerked up—landing, unfortunately, on that full, lush mouth, outlined at that moment in lollipop-pink. He had never forgotten how that mouth had felt under his. How she'd tasted. And smelt. He imagined her whole body would be like one of those delicious lollipops which you licked and licked, and hoped never ran out.

Ben's eyes were angry by the time they lifted to

hers. But it was anger at himself. He hated his sexual vulnerability to her. Hated it!

Amber could not believe she just stood there, letting him look her over like that. With such an insulting mixture of derision and desire. Worse was her own involuntary physical reaction. Her heart pounded. Her blood began to boil.

But not in temper.

God, but she was hopeless where Ben was concerned. Or was it *help*less? What would happen, she worried, if he were to take her in his arms even now? What would she do? The thought terrified yet fascinated her. Already she could feel her face flushing with an unbidden excitement, which only seemed to increase his contempt for her.

'Caught you red-handed, didn't I?' he mocked, on straightening. 'Or should I say…red-faced.'

Amber's high colour quickly retreated in response to his scorn. 'I don't know what you mean.'

Ben laughed. 'I have to admire you, Amber. You're always at your best when you should be cringing with shame. You know damned well I said to be here at four, yet you arrive an hour earlier, no doubt hoping to ingratiate yourself with Gran somehow before I've had a chance to speak to her.'

'The day hasn't dawned when I would cringe with shame in front of you, Ben Sinclair,' she said, her voice and manner carrying disdain as she walked round to the passenger side of her car. But her hands were shaking as she wrenched open the car door and scooped up the cardboard box containing the apple tea cake she'd brought with her.

Damn the man! What right did he have to judge her so harshly when his behaviour that night had been just as reprehensible as her own?

And what right did he have to still be so damned attractive to her? He wasn't all that good-looking, really. She'd met far more handsome men. With far more perfect profiles. And far more beautiful bodies. But one insolent look from those darkly passionate eyes of his and she could hardly think straight.

It wasn't fair. It just wasn't fair!

Amber slammed the car door and glared at him over the bonnet. 'I couldn't remember exactly what time you said after you hung up on me so rudely last night,' she snapped. 'I could only recall you said mid-afternoon. *This* is mid-afternoon. I was hoping—foolishly I can see—that you would give me a decent hearing today. But I see you're still so full of petty grievances and grudges that you won't even give me a chance.

'Still, I shouldn't have expected any more of you. You always were possessed of a boorish disposition. You could only ever see your own selfish point of view, Ben Sinclair, and I see you haven't changed a bit!'

The noise of his Gran's old wire door creaking open

then banging shut stopped Ben from having to defend himself after Amber's tirade.

Which was just as well. Because Amber had touched quite a few nerves with her attack. And made him feel oddly guilty over his past treatment of her. Ben was at a weird loss for words, so he was relieved to turn his attention to his gran—till he saw she was hobbling down the front steps with the help of a walking stick.

What on earth was she doing with a walking stick? Had she had a fall? Was she suffering from rheumatism or arthritis?

Ben didn't know. All he knew was that suddenly she looked every one of her seventy-nine years. And more. Her normally wiry body seemed extra frail beneath the cheap floral dress. Her frizzy grey hair badly needed a perm. The trainers on her feet were dirty and scuffed.

Her general image was one of neglect and advancing age. His heart contracted at the sight of her, and her obvious decline since his last visit. Frustration that she would never take any of his money mingled with remorse that he hadn't come home at Christmas. He could feel Amber's eyes upon him, and knew she had been right in some of her accusations. He *was* selfish. Why hadn't he realised his gran would have been hurt by his not coming home? That she would have been awfully lonely?

His heart sank. Oh, Gran… Forgive me.

She stopped at that moment, and looked up at him,

her dark eyes twinkling, but her wrinkled mouth pursed into an expression of grandmotherly reproach.

'Ben Sinclair,' she said sternly. 'Why didn't you tell me you were coming?' And she held out her one free arm towards him.

Ben's heart lurched as he vaulted over the rickety iron gate and swiftly covered the ground that separated him from the one person in his life whose unfailing love had never let him down.

A distressing jealousy took possession of Amber as she watched Ben hug his gran, watched him hold her tight. It gripped her deep inside her chest, constricting her heart and bringing a very real pain. She wasn't sure if she envied their ability to demonstrate their closeness in a physical fashion, or if her jealousy was due to that awful inner yearning which had never really left her to have Ben finish what he had once started. How many times over the years had she dreamt of his making love to her? Not up against some hard wooden door, but in a bed, against satin sheets, and at his leisure...

'Hard to tell you I was coming,' the man himself was saying as he let his gran go. 'According to the phone company, you've taken the phone off the hook.'

'But I haven't!' Pearl protested. 'I.... Oh...oh, yes, I did take it off the hook the other night for a little while. I must have forgotten to put it back on. I...er...seem to be getting a little forgetful lately.'

Amber frowned. She would not have said Pearl Sinclair was at all forgetful, but maybe she was being unfair to the old lady. She looked a lot more fragile than she had the other day. And she was using a walking stick. Amber was sure there hadn't been a walking stick last Monday. Still, what was the old dear? Nearly eighty? Amber supposed it was only natural that at eighty years of age some days would be better than others.

'Why did you do that, Gran?' Ben questioned. 'Been getting some crank calls, have you?'

Pearl looked taken aback. 'What…what do you mean?'

'I've seen the local paper, Gran. I have it sent to me every week. I thought you knew that.'

'Oh. I…I forgot…'

'Why didn't you call me and tell me what was going on?'

'I…I didn't want to bother you. I know how busy you are down there in Sydney. And it's *my* problem, after all,' she finished defiantly.

'When my Gran starts getting crank calls, then it becomes *my* business.'

'Yes, well, there was only the one,' she said, looking a little embarrassed at the fuss her grandson was making.

Amber was touched by their relationship. It was obvious Ben loved his grandmother very much. And more than obvious she thought the world of him in return, and probably missed him like mad.

But she was a proud old lady. Too proud to beg him to visit more often. Far too proud to ask him for help.

Not that this matter really needed Ben's help.

It was becoming blown out of all proportion in Amber's opinion. Next thing, he'd accuse *her* of making that crank call, of harassing the poor old dear instead of trying to give her enough money and some added bonuses which would set her up for a very comfortable retirement.

Amber stood on the other side of the gate, feeling very uncomfortable. She was sure Mrs Sinclair could see her standing there, but the old lady was deliberately ignoring her presence, as was Ben for the moment.

'So what did this crank caller say?' he asked.

'What? Oh…er…nothing much, really.'

'Gran, don't mess me around. Tell me.'

'But I couldn't repeat what he said, Ben.'

'So it was a man? And he swore at you?'

'I've never heard so many four-letter words!'

'So what was the general thrust of what he said?'

'He was telling me to get out or else…' At last she glared over Ben's shoulder at Amber.

Ben saw the direction of his gran's gaze and turned to frown at Amber, who was trying not to look stupid, just standing there holding a tea cake.

'Or else what?' he ground out.

'He didn't say, exactly.'

'But he frightened you enough to take the phone off the hook,' Ben surmised aloud.

Amber decided enough was enough!

'Hollingsworths had nothing to do with that crank call, Mrs Sinclair,' she insisted, totally ignoring Ben's glower. 'We don't do things that way. My guess is that the story in the paper got some people riled up who might have found jobs building the complex. It's an unfortunate fact of life that, once the media are involved, things like this happen.'

'What's *she* doing here, Ben?' Pearl said sharply.

'I asked her to come, Gran,' he admitted.

'Why?'

'When I couldn't get through to you, I rang Amber to find out what was going on. She wanted the chance to speak to you again, and I decided this was best done while I was here.'

'Hmph! I would have thought that was the last thing on earth you'd have wanted,' the old lady grumbled. 'From what I've gathered over the years there's no love lost between you two. Never has been.'

'Yes, well, that was in the past, Gran,' Ben astonished Amber by saying. 'And this is the present. We're both adults now, and I think it's time we acted like adults—don't you, Amber?'

Her eyebrows shot skywards. Was she hearing right? Was that Ben Sinclair saying he wanted to let bygones be bygones? You could have knocked her over with a feather. 'Well...er...um...' Amber stammered. She felt totally flummoxed, even more so when Ben suddenly smiled at her.

Admittedly, it was a rather rueful smile, but it showed that he didn't always have to look so fierce, or angry. Smiling brought a touch of warmth to his cruelly sculptured mouth, plus an amused gleam to those jet-black eyes, which usually chilled her with their arctic coldness.

'That's the second time in as many days I've rendered you speechless,' Ben said, sarcasm back in his voice. 'I have to admit I prefer you that way. But it will make the delivering of your new sales pitch decidedly awkward, don't you think? Shall we ask her inside, Gran, and hear what she's got to say?'

'Won't make no difference,' Pearl pronounced quite cheerfully. 'I'm not selling. So whatcha got there, girlie?' the old lady asked, pointing her walking stick at the box in Amber's arms.

'A tea cake,' Amber admitted.

Pearl pursed her lips, her expression thoughtful. 'One of them ones with apple in the middle?'

Amber tried not to smile as she said, 'The one and the same.'

'Mmm. In that case you'd better come inside. I've always been a sucker for a tea cake with apple in the middle.'

Ben arched an eyebrow at Amber drily, suggesting that he guessed this wasn't an accident, that she'd made it her business to find out what might get her back into his gran's good books, or at least smooth the way back into her kitchen.

Amber put her hand on the front gate, then hesitated. It was with a barely hidden spark of mischief that she glanced around with feigned agitation. 'Are you sure it's all right for me to come inside the gate?' she asked. 'I mean…isn't that killer dog of yours on the loose somewhere?'

Pearl's eyes narrowed while Ben's widened, as though he'd had no idea up till then that Amber had such a wicked sense of humour.

'You taking the mickey out of me, girlie?' his gran snapped.

Amber hadn't been cast in the lead in their high school play for nothing. 'Golly, no, ma'am. But I know dogs can sense fear in a person, and after what you said in the paper I'm scared to death of that big old greyhound of yours. Rocky, you said he was called?'

As though on cue, but perhaps because he'd heard his name, the dog himself bounded out through the wire door, launching his roly-poly frame down the steps and along the front path. Totally ignoring his mistress and her grandson, he jumped up at the gate, putting his big paws on top, his huge, slobbery pink tongue lolling out the side of his big grinning choppers. Not a bark in sight, let alone a bite. He was obviously dying for Amber to give him a scratch behind the ears—which activity had occupied most of her stay the other day, when Rocky had grovelled at her feet for her entire visit.

Amber carefully moved the fragile cardboard box into the crook of her left arm, freeing her right hand to satisfy the dog's craving. Rocky practically sighed his pleasure when Amber began, at which his mistress also sighed.

'I should have let them send that useless mutt to the knackers',' she mumbled. 'Or wherever useless greyhounds go. All right, Miss Smartypants, you've made your point. Ben, drag that drooling idiot away and let our visitor in. I'll go put on the kettle. But don't go thinking the dog reflects the feelings of the management,' she warned, before turning her back and making her way inside—much more quickly than she'd emerged, Amber noted.

'Traitor,' Ben muttered to the dog as he grabbed its collar and wrenched him away from Amber's touch. 'Inside,' he ordered, and the dog bolted after his mistress with all his usual courage.

'It's nice to see that not all those living at the Sinclair farm despise us Hollingsworths,' Amber could not resist saying. 'Aren't dogs and children supposed to be able to judge a person's character better than other adults?'

Ben smiled again. But there was little warmth in it. And any amusement was decidedly hard-edged. 'Are you suggesting I might have misjudged you all these years, Amber?'

'I'm suggesting you might give credence to the possibility that I've changed.'

'Really? How intriguing. Here, give me that box before you drop it.' He took it out of her arms across the gate, then did the strangest thing. He put it on the ground. Before she knew what he had in mind, he was cupping her face and kissing her across the gate.

She let her lips part under the pressure of his without thinking, and when his tongue darted forth to contact hers she made a small whimpering sound of dazed pleasure.

Ben's mouth immediately lifted, leaving her to stare up at him with wide eyes. Gradually she saw that he was glaring at her with every ounce of his old contempt.

'See?' he drawled. 'You haven't changed a bit.'

No, Amber realised wretchedly as the full horror of what he'd just done sank in, along with the horror of her own appalling weakness in surrendering herself to him again. Instantly. Instinctively.

But this time she could not pretend to be unaffected. She could not conjure up an icy shell to withdraw behind, or find some counter-barb to cut him down to size.

Tears filled her eyes. Tears of utter misery. For a minute there today, she'd thought—and hoped—that they *might* be able to put the past behind them and go forward. That they might even become friends.

Amber swallowed the huge lump of hurt that was filling her throat and somehow found her voice.

'Please tell your grandmother that I hope she enjoys the tea cake, but I think it best I go home now. I can see I'm wasting my time here,' she finished in strangled tones.

Whirling, she hurried over and into her car, battling to clear her blurred gaze as she slammed the door and reached for the ignition. She ignored Ben's shout for her to wait, and reversed out at speed, almost side-swiping his car as her own slewed around to face the right way. She put her foot to the floor, the tyres screeching as she careered off.

The rear vision mirror showed Ben racing through the cloud of dust she'd left behind to stand in the middle of the road, staring after her.

'Bastard,' she choked out, and thumped the steering wheel. 'Bastard!'

CHAPTER FIVE

BEN muttered an expletive under his breath. Then another. And another.

His remorse was as intense as his self-loathing. Who in hell did he think he was to do such a contemptible thing?

Okay, so she'd responded to his kiss. With stunning speed and quite astonishing ardour. But so what? He had no right to condemn her for what he'd done himself in the past. How many times had he found pleasure in the mouths of women he didn't exactly respect, let alone like?

Ben could forgive himself for throwing Amber's highly sexed nature in her face when he'd been an emotionally involved teenager. But such despicable double standards were now simply not acceptable.

Hell, he couldn't get the hurt on her face out of his mind. Ben, you should be hung, drawn and quartered. No one deserves to be treated like that—not even Amber Hollingsworth!

'Ben!' came his gran's call from the verandah. 'What are you doing standing in the middle of the road out there? And where's Miss Hollingsworth?'

Ben sighed and walked slowly back through the open gate before bending to scoop up the box from where he'd put it not two minutes earlier. Two miserable minutes. But how he wished he could go back and relive them! Then he would definitely not give in to that despicable urge which had overtaken him to kiss her and prove...what, for pity's sake? That she was a promiscuous trollop who wasn't worth losing sleep over?

He shook his head as he made his way wearily along the front path. Maybe he'd been trying to prove that he was over her at last, that he could kiss her and remain unmoved by the full softness of her lips and the luscious curves of her woman's body.

Yet all he'd proved was the opposite. She could move him now as much as ever. Not just physically, either. She'd moved more than his flesh this time. She'd moved his emotions, made him feel regret and remorse, made him want to say how sorry he was, made him despise himself for hurting her.

'Ben?' his gran queried as he walked up the front steps, box in hand. 'Ben, what happened? What did you do?'

'What did I do?' he echoed unhappily. 'I insulted her, Gran. That's what I did.'

'Yes, well, that's nothing new, is it? That's been the way between you two for as long as I can remember. Never a civil word to say to each other. But she usually gives as good as she gets, that girl. What made her take off like a scalded cat?'

Ben sighed. 'I guess I went too far, Gran.'

Her eyebrows lifted. 'In what way?'

Ben decided he'd said enough. 'Just drop it, will you? After all, I got rid of her, didn't I? Isn't that what you said you wanted in the paper? To be left alone by the Hollingsworths?'

Ben detected alarm in his gran's face. 'Are you saying she won't be coming back? At *all*?'

'For Pete's sake, make up your mind,' he said irritably. 'You either want to sell this place or you don't!' A thought infiltrated which didn't please him at all. 'Good grief, Gran, that business in the paper wasn't a ploy to get more money out of the Hollingsworths, was it?' He had never thought of his gran as mercenary, but all of a sudden something smelt about this whole thing.

'Not at all!' she protested indignantly.

His eyes narrowed when his gran wouldn't look him in the eye. She wasn't telling him the truth. At least...not the whole truth and nothing but the truth.

'You're up to something,' he told her.

'Don't be silly,' she denied. 'What could I possibly be up to?'

'I don't know. Yet.'

'You have a suspicious nature, Ben Sinclair. And you're far too quick to believe badly of people.'

Amber rushed back into his mind and he scowled. 'Maybe, but you can't talk. It's a case of the pot calling the kettle black, I think.'

'Speaking of kettles, mine must be boiling away like mad by now.'

'Dear Lord, surely you're not still boiling water on

that old combustion stove? I sent you a nice new electric jug for Christmas.' Not to mention a microwave and an automatic toaster. Christmas and birthdays were the only occasions on which Ben could indulge his wish to repay his gran in some way. Even then, he knew there was a limit to how much she would accept, but he'd thought he was safe with kitchen appliances.

Ben followed his gran down the hallway, slipping the telephone back on the hook on the way past. He could hear the kettle hissing before they reached the kitchen door. Pearl hurried over and took it off the blackened stove-top while Ben put the tea cake on the kitchen table and glanced around. All his gifts were lined up proudly on a dresser-top against the wall, but none had even been unpacked, let alone used.

'Gran, you haven't even taken the electric kettle out of the box. Or any of the other appliances I gave you, for that matter.'

'I know,' she sighed. 'Just can't get the hang of the instruction books which come with them new-fandangled gadgets. Now don't go mad on me, Ben. I really do appreciate all the things you bought me. You're a thoughtful boy. But it's hard to teach an old dog new tricks.'

'You seem to have done a good job with Rocky there,' Ben returned drily, nodding towards the greyhound, whose fat bulk was stretched out under the kitchen table. 'For a racing dog who was branded a fighter, he's sure turned over a new leaf.'

Pearl chuckled. 'Made a right fool of me with Amber, didn't he?'

'Don't take it to heart, Gran. A lot of males have been made fools of by Amber Hollingsworth.'

'Does that include you?' Pearl asked while she busied herself with tea-making.

'Afraid so,' Ben admitted.

'Well, she's a mighty pretty girl.'

'Not so much a girl any longer. She must be twenty-eight, at least. With a husband behind her, and God knows how many lovers. Amber's not the type to ever be without a boyfriend.'

'Really? Well, I haven't heard her name connected with any man around town. And you know Sunrise. A girl's only got to stop on a street corner and talk to an eligible chappy and she's going to bed with him.'

Ben knew that was the case, but he couldn't imagine Amber not having a lover. Not for three whole years!

'Sit down, for heaven's sake,' Pearl said, coming over to the table with the tea-tray. She placed it on the ancient formica-topped table then lifted the lid off the cardboard box. 'My, that is one delicious looking tea cake! A few calories there, I'll warrant. Still, you look like you could do with some decent food,' she went on as she cut it into slices. 'Doesn't that city girlfriend of yours look after you, Ben?'

Ben rolled his eyes. This was a standard complaint every time he came home. That he wasn't eating properly. Yet he'd been the same weight for as long as he could remember.

'I live alone, Gran, as you very well know,' he said with a sigh, scraping out one of the battered wooden chairs and sitting down.

'That Brenda hasn't moved in with you?'

'God, no.' What a horrible thought!

Pearl poured the tea, frowning. 'But I thought you'd be getting married soon. You went to meet her parents at Christmas, didn't you?'

'Not really.'

'Oh...my mistake, then.'

'No, *my* mistake, Gran. I should have come home and spent Christmas with you. It would have been much more fun. Not only that, I missed you.'

Ben was touched by the shimmer of tears which misted his gran's eyes, even though she tried not to let him see them by looking down and blinking like mad. 'I missed you too, love,' she said softly. 'But you're home now...'

'Yes. I am. And while I'm here I think we should talk very seriously about the Hollingsworths' offer. I know you said you didn't want to sell. And that was my first reaction, too. But you're not getting any younger, Gran, and this place is very run-down. You certainly won't ever get a better offer than the Hollingsworths'. You could buy a very nice little place closer to town with what they'll pay you, and have a good deal left over for whatever luxury takes your fancy.'

'I've never set much store by luxuries,' Pearl said, and sat down.

Ben reached over and covered one of her wrinkled, sun-spotted hands with his smooth, tanned fingers. 'But do you really want to stay here for ever, Gran? You're not just being stubborn for the hell of it, are you?'

She pulled her hand away and lifted her chin. 'I have a right to be stubborn if I want to be! And I've a right to live out my days wherever I want.'

The telephone jangled, and Gran jumped in her chair. Ben could see the surprise in her instantly rounded eyes. Or was it fear?

'It's all right, Gran,' he reassured her. 'I'll answer it.'

He pushed back his chair, stood up then strode out of the kitchen and down the hallway to where the telephone sat on its rickety old stand, ringing its head off as though it were angry for having been out of action for so long. Ben scooped the receiver up to his ear.

'Now listen 'ere, you stupid old bag!' a rough male voice snarled, before he could utter a single word. 'Get that scrawny hide of yours out of there before someone does it for you—lock, stock and barrel! You've got one week to sell up and bloody well clear out. If you don't, you won't have a house left worth living in. Savvy?'

Ben barely got his mouth open before the oh, so

polite caller hung up, the bang reverberating down to his eardrum.

'Damn and blast!' he muttered, then hung up himself, outrage warring with an escalating fury. He hoped it was a coincidence that the call had come shortly after Amber would have returned home and told her father of her failure to clinch the sale. Had that loud-mouthed father of hers called one of his henchmen to put some pressure on? Or was it one of the locals, resenting an old lady standing in the way of work opportunities?

'Was that Amber?' Pearl asked from the kitchen doorway.

'No,' Ben snapped. 'It was another of those crank calls. Hung up before I could give him a piece of my mind.'

His gran paled at the news, making Ben wish he'd had the quick thinking to make up a little white lie. Hell, she looked as if she was going to faint.

'What…what did he say?' she asked shakily as he helped her back into the kitchen and into her chair, taking the opposite one for himself.

'Pretty well the same as last time, I guess. Sell up and get out or else.'

'Oh, my!' Her hands fluttered up to her heart.

'Are you all right?' Ben asked worriedly.

'I…I just didn't realise…'

'That people could be so damned awful?' Ben finished for her. 'Welcome to the real world.'

'No, it…it's not that. It's just that I…I…'

'What?'

'Oh, nothing. It's too late now.'

'It's not too late to sell, if that's what you really want to do.'

'Sell? Just because some bully boy rings up and shouts his mouth off? Not on your life! Bullies never really do anything, anyway. They're all talk!'

Ben didn't agree with that theory at all. In his experience bullies very often did a lot more than just talk, but he didn't want to frighten his gran by saying so. He hadn't realised just how much ill feeling her story in the paper might stir up. Neither had he realised Sunrise had such an unemployment problem till he'd seen the evidence for himself.

Really, the safest and probably the best solution all round would be to convince her to sell. He'd offer to take her back to Sydney to live with him. He could easily sell his unit and buy a nice little house. In a beachside suburb, perhaps. Gran had always wanted to live nearer the water.

But he wouldn't mention these plans to her tonight. He'd give her a day or so for the reality of the situation to sink in. Meanwhile...

'Excuse me, Gran,' he said, 'but I think I'd best take that phone back off the hook.'

'But what if Amber tries to ring you?'

'You have to be joking. That's the last thing Amber will do.'

'Well, what if she tries to ring me?'

As if responding to mental telepathy, the telephone

did ring precisely at that moment. Ben knew, however, that it wasn't Amber. Crank callers had a history of persistence.

'Right!' he ground out, pressing balled fists against the table-top to launch himself out of the chair.

'Ben, don't you go swearing!' his gran called out after him as he marched towards the hall. 'There's no need to bring yourself down to other people's level!'

Personally, Ben didn't subscribe to *that* little theory, either. There were times when coming down to other people's level was the only way. Certain sub-human species didn't understand civility. Or decency. All they understood was a good smack in the mouth. Since he wasn't able to deliver that over the telephone, he would have to revert to verbal rather than physical abuse. Not as effective, but beggars couldn't be choosers!

'Now, you look here, you scumbag!' he roared down the line, simultaneously sweeping the receiver up to his mouth. 'If I catch you coming anywhere near my gran or her house you're going to look like you've done fifteen rounds with Mike Tyson. I'll have you know that making harassing calls is a jailable offence under new laws. The police can also now trace a call within seconds,' he invented, 'so if you value your miserable hide you'll get off this line and stay off! In fact, I suggest you get out of Sunrise and stay out, if you know what's good for you!'

Ben waited for the sound of the offender to hang up in fright. Instead, there was a brief silence on the other end of the line, before a hoity-toity female voice said, with great restraint and considerable understatement, 'I presume that is Ben Sinclair? Obviously you thought I was someone else, but this is Beverly Hollingsworth speaking. Edward Hollingsworth's wife and Amber's stepmother.'

Ben closed his eyes for a second, grateful that the heated colour rushing into his cheeks could not be seen by anyone. He contemplated apologising profusely, but then decided that any woman who could tolerate such a barrage with such cool aplomb did not need kid-glove treatment. He had never met Beverly Hollingsworth, but he would imagine any woman who had married Edward Hollingsworth would not be some hot-house flower type.

His judgement was quickly confirmed by the cool way she swept on. 'I am calling to ask you if you would be kind enough to join the family for dinner tomorrow evening. My husband has certain business matters he would like to discuss with you, but unfortunately, since his illness, he is unable to leave the house.'

'No trouble, Mrs Hollingsworth,' Ben returned super-suavely. 'I would be delighted to accept your invitation to dinner.'

'Wonderful. Shall we say seven-thirty?'

'I'll be there right on the dot.'

'Excellent. And might I add how much I'm looking forward to meeting you, Mr Sinclair? I've heard so much about you.'

'Really? How flattering.'

'Oh, no. None of it was at all flattering.' A malicious little laugh floated down the line. 'You seem to have got under my stepdaughter's skin, for some reason or other. She came home this afternoon and refused, point-blank, to tell her father what went on between you two. She just said she couldn't do business with you any more, then went straight to her room. Could you possibly enlighten me on the situation?'

Ben decided he didn't like Beverly Hollingsworth one little bit. 'I think Amber may have misunderstood something I said. But, if you're speaking to her, please tell her from me that I'm sorry and that I am looking forward to seeing her tomorrow evening.'

'How sweet.'

'Oh, no,' he parodied with ill-concealed sarcasm. 'Nothing about me is at all sweet, Mrs Hollingsworth. Till tomorrow evening, then,' he finished, and hung up.

His gran gave him a speculative look as he walked slowly back into the kitchen.

He smiled a wry smile. 'Looks like I jumped the gun, Gran. It wasn't our resident crank caller at all. It was Mrs Beverly Hollingsworth.'

'Oh, my...'

'Exactly. But all's well that ends well. I've been invited to the Hollingsworths' for dinner tomorrow evening. Amber's father is obviously going to make me an offer that you shouldn't refuse. What do you think of that?'

It looked as if she thought it was a very good idea.

'Something tells me you're not as against the idea of selling as you've been making out, Gran.'

'It's always a woman's privilege to change her mind. Just you remember that.'

'Is there some particular point you're making with that remark?'

'Do stop sounding like you're in court, Ben.'

'Sorry.'

'So you should be. All I'm saying is that just because Amber didn't like you much when she was a teenager, it doesn't mean she hasn't a different opinion altogether now that she's all grown up. I had quite a long chat with her the other day, and you've no idea how often she turned the conversation around to a certain man who shall remain nameless but who works as a lawyer in Sydney and drives a nice black car.'

Ben's stomach flipped right over at what his gran was implying. Could it be true? Could Amber's feelings for him be deeper than he'd ever imagined? Or hoped?

Such a hope did things to him that were as telling as they were frightening.

The realisation that he might have been in love with Amber all these years brought with it an immediate and fierce denial.

Of course you're not in love with her, you fool, he told himself sternly. And she is not even remotely in love with you!

Ben swiftly reverted to a far more safe belief: that what he'd thrown at Amber earlier that afternoon was still true. She still fancied him sexually, but she didn't like him any more than she ever had. And it was the same with him. It *had* to be. Anything else was fraught with such potentially heartbreaking possibilities that he simply refused to embrace them. It wasn't love that moved him whenever he looked at Amber. It was another four-letter word starting with L, and with which he was far more comfortable.

He laughed. But even to his own ears he sounded shaken.

'Laugh if you like,' his gran said airily, and slid a big slice of tea cake in front of him. 'But you'll laugh on the other side of your face one day, I'll warrant, Ben Sinclair!'

Ben didn't doubt the wisdom of his gran's words. He just hoped that the day of his downfall wasn't tomorrow evening at the Hollingsworths'!

CHAPTER SIX

AMBER was lying on her bed when her stepmother came into her room. Without knocking. It was just after four, and less than an hour since Amber's upsetting encounter with Ben.

'You know, Amber,' Beverly began tersely, 'I think you were right about that Ben Sinclair. He *is* a bastard. But you were wrong about his accepting my dinner invitation. He said yes straight away.'

Amber closed her eyes. She could not believe that Beverly had actually invited Ben to dinner. And she could not believe that he was coming.

There could only be one explanation, and her heart sank with the acceptance that her father had been right all along. That article in the paper shouting scandal had all been a scam to get more money out of them.

Amber's dismay was intense. She knew Ben could be ruthless, but not his grandmother. It was hard to believe that the old lady was nothing but a greedy, grasping partner in such underhanded and conscienceless tactics.

'Oh, I see,' her stepmother went on waspishly. 'I'm to be subjected to the silent treatment. How charming. I suppose you're not interested in hearing that your Mr Sinclair also expressed his apologies for whatever it was he said to upset you today, and hoped you would be there at dinner tomorrow night?'

Shock sprung open Amber's eyes. She sat up and swung her legs over the side of her bed, then looked up at her stepmother, frowning her astonishment. 'Ben *apologised*?' That was not the sort of thing Ben would do. Never! Not even for money.

At least...she hadn't thought so prior to today.

'I've got your attention now, have I?' Beverly sniped. 'My, this Ben must be really something to have captured *your* interest. And he's not even rich!'

Amber sighed. 'You have the wrong idea about me, Beverly.'

'I don't think so. I think I have you taped perfectly.'

'Do you?' Amber stood up and walked over to the bedroom window, which looked down over the valley and the town. 'You know nothing about me,' she murmured. 'Nothing...'

'In that case surprise me by being at dinner tomorrow night. Do something for your father for once! Or was that tantrum this afternoon the forerunner of your running away from life again? I dare say you've grown tired of playing businesswoman now that your pet project hasn't been all smooth sailing. Or is it that you can't stand to see your father succeed where you failed? Because he'll get that arrogant boyfriend of yours to persuade his grandmother to sell tomorrow night—you mark my words!'

'Ben might be arrogant but he is not my boyfriend,'

Amber told her coolly. 'Never has been and never will be.'

'Ah, so that's the reason behind your peculiar antagonism towards him. Dear Ben isn't one of the many blind fools who once threw themselves at the beautiful Amber Hollingsworth's feet.'

Amber smiled a rueful smile. 'Well, you've got that last bit right, at least. But you're wrong about the rest. If ever I leave this house it will be *you* I'm running away from, Beverly, not life. And certainly not Ben Sinclair. Neither am I jealous of Dad's business skills. I sincerely hope, for the town's sake, that he does succeed where I failed. I can't imagine my being at the dinner will increase his chances of success, but if he wants me there I'll be quite happy to attend.'

'You won't go back on that?' Beverly snapped.

'Why should I?'

'Because of Ben Sinclair, that's why. You said you didn't want anything more to do with him.'

'That was before he apologised,' she said with an indifferent shrug. And before it became a matter of personal pride and survival, she thought, holding her stepmother's cold eyes with all the nonchalance she could muster. Beverly had seen a chink in Amber's armour this afternoon and had really gone in for the kill. Amber suspected tomorrow night's dinner would be another arena in which Beverly would try to do battle with her stepdaughter.

Amber resolved, if not to win, then to come through as unscathed as possible. On top of that, she *was* curious over Ben's apology. Her earlier conclusions over Ben being in a scam for money just didn't feel right. Neither did his ready acceptance of the dinner invitation. She certainly wanted to be there to hear what he had to say when her father made a more lucrative offer for the farm.

Which he would.

'Promise me you won't make some sort of scene while he's here,' Beverly persisted.

'I wouldn't dream of it.'

Beverly's laugh was ugly with sarcasm. 'That butter-won't-melt-in-your-mouth routine doesn't fool me for a minute. You were livid with him when you arrived home. And you're still stewing over something. I'd love to know what he did or said to upset you so much.'

Amber was not about to tell her stepmother that Ben had reduced her to jelly with a five-second kiss and then flung his old accusation in her face: that she was a promiscuous trollop who would open her legs for anyone at the drop of a hat. He hadn't said as much in so many words, of course. But that was what he'd meant when he'd said she hadn't changed.

She pondered that kiss again, from the safety of distance, and worried that Ben might be right about her sexual weakness. But only where *he* was concerned. She'd never been easy with other men. She'd resisted Chris's advances when they'd been dating. And she hadn't slept with Chad till their wedding night.

God, what a nightmare that marriage had been! She hated thinking about it.

After leaving Chad, she hadn't wanted anything to do with another relationship. Sex never entered her mind now, except on the odd occasion when she ran into Ben. After seeing him she would lie in bed at night and think about it all the time. It was only by burying herself in work that she would finally rout those disturbing urges, both from her brain and her body.

If there was any danger in having dinner with Ben tomorrow night, it was not that she would disgrace her father and stepmother by acting like a shrew, but rather that she would sit there in a silent ferment of desire, thinking about how it would feel to have Ben kiss her all over.

That train of thought was a mistake. Amber clenched her jaw hard and tried to stop her traitorous heartbeat from picking up speed.

'Sorry to disappoint you, Beverly,' she said abruptly, 'but I don't want to discuss Ben Sinclair any more. I've said I'll be there at the dinner. Now, if you don't mind, I'm going to run myself a bath.'

Beverly opened then shut her mouth, as though she'd been going to try one last parting barb then thought better of it. 'You do that, dear,' she said with a saccharine smile. 'I'll go and tell your father you'll be at the dinner. He'll be most pleased, I'm sure.'

Amber sighed once the door was safely shut. Things were becoming intolerable with Beverly, she accepted. It was time she found somewhere else to live.

Yet she didn't want to leave Sunrise. People might have thought that all those years of tripping around the world with her wealthy, jet-setting husband would have given her a feel for the high life. Or at least city life. Instead, it had made her want something far simpler. It had made her want to come home to the small coastal town she'd been born and brought up in. She could still remember her first reaction on driving back into town three years ago. She'd had to pull over and stop, she'd been crying so much.

No, no one was going to run her out of town. Not even the wicked witch of a stepmother Beverly had unexpectedly turned into.

Amber immediately thought of the cottage which was part of the new exchange package for the farm she'd been going to offer Pearl Sinclair that afternoon. It had three bedrooms, a lovely garden and a pleasant view of the ocean from its position on top of a hill.

It was a deceased estate, and Hollingsworths had bought the house and its contents for a song the previous month. When she'd taken over as managing director, Amber had instructed the manager of their real estate section to always keep an eye out for any local bargain, and he'd been cockahoop about this purchase. At the time, he'd happily informed Amber that all the furniture, though old-fashioned, was quality stuff. His suggestion had been that they auction the contents, then have the house repainted before reselling it.

But when Amber had visited the property she hadn't wanted to do that. The furniture fitted the cosy weatherboard cottage, and the effect as a whole was charming. In the back of her mind she'd imagined that she might live in it herself one day. Meantime, her plan had been to rent it out as a furnished dwelling, though a suitable tenant had not yet been found. When Amber had wanted a carrot to dangle in front of Pearl Sinclair, she'd immediately thought of the cottage.

Now she thought of it again…as a place to live in herself—not at some time in the mythical future, but now. She couldn't bear to live under the same roof as Beverly for another moment. First thing in the morning she would drive over there and see what she had to buy before she could move in.

It would be good for her to keep busy tomorrow. The devil, they said, made work for idle hands. And idle minds, she added. Even now devilishly tempting thoughts were crowding back in. Thoughts of Ben's body all those years ago, fused with hers. Thoughts of the way he'd looked her over today, undressing her with his eyes.

And then there had been that kiss, which had been not so much a kiss as an oral insult. And yet their lips had moulded to each other's for those few brief moments, and she realised, in retrospect, that he'd been as aroused by the contact as she had been. He might still despise her, but he also desired her. *He* hadn't changed in that respect, either.

Amber hugged herself and shivered. Would they never be done with one another?

Probably not, she finally conceded. Not while there was breath in her body, and in his. There was a dark bonding between them which defied common sense, plus their consciences. A love/hate relationship which would undoubtedly follow them to the grave.

Amber was startled by the intensity of emotion her thoughts had conjured up. Love? Hate? Were their feelings really as deep as that?

Maybe his weren't. But hers definitely were. It frightened her to admit it, but she could so easily fall in love with Ben. She suspected it would only take one gentle gesture, a sweet smile, a seemingly sincere apology, and all her defences would crumble.

She prayed and hoped that none of those things would ever happen, that he would continue to insult and deride her. Because to fall in love with Ben Sinclair would be to court a disaster even worse than her marriage to Chad. At least Chad had loved her, in his own weird, warped way.

But Ben Sinclair would never love her back, not as she wanted and needed to be loved. For there was no compassion in him. No softness. No kindness. Never had been and never would be.

Amber did not realise she was crying till the tears ran into the corners of her mouth. Angrily she dashed the tears away, and, whirling, stalked across her bedroom and into her private bathroom.

'Damn you, Ben Sinclair!' she muttered as she snapped on the bath taps. 'Damn you to hell!'

CHAPTER SEVEN

THE Hollingsworth home was impressive, perched on the crest of a hill, with a commanding view of the valley and the town below. It was two-storeyed, wide and white, with dark green shutters at the windows. The front porch and upper balcony were supported by four white columns, and the front door was flanked by two matching ornamental fig trees in large green pots.

Ben drew up at the front steps of the house a minute before seven-thirty on the Saturday evening. Daylight saving meant the sun had not yet set, though it was rapidly sinking behind the mountainous horizon.

Thank heavens, Ben thought as he climbed out.

The day had been exceptionally hot, especially for early March. Humid as well. Ben's shirt was sticking to his back as he climbed out of his car. At moments like this he regretted buying a black car. Despite the very efficient air-conditioning in his Saab, it was still a hot colour, especially when the car had been sitting in the sun all afternoon, waiting to have a wheel alignment.

Ben hoped he didn't look as hot and bothered as he felt as he walked up the front steps. Whatever had possessed him to accept this blessed invitation? There was simply no point to his being here. Gran still stubbornly refused to even consider selling the farm. He had no power to negotiate any new offer on her behalf. Nor would he promise Edward Hollingsworth to try to persuade her to sell against her expressed wishes.

So why *was* he here? Why hadn't he rung and cancelled the dinner once Gran made her feelings quite clear over lunch?

He told himself that it was in part because Gran thought it was a good idea for him to come and see the lie of the land for himself. But the real reason behind his presence—and his agitated state—went by the name of Amber Hollingsworth.

'You're a masochist, Ben Sinclair,' he whispered to himself as he reached up and rang the doorbell.

It chimed a musical message to whoever's job it was to answer the door. He doubted it would be the daughter of the house, which was somewhat of a relief. He wasn't quite ready for Amber yet.

The woman who answered the door was clearly Mrs Edward Hollingsworth. In the flesh.

She'd once been pretty, Ben imagined. Around fifty years of age, she was now carrying far too many pounds for her small frame. But she had superbly styled blonde hair, and was wearing a cleverly draped pink dress which must have cost a fortune. A wide pearl choker covered some of the wrinkles in her neck. Huge pearl-drop earrings dangled from her ears.

'Why, Mr Sinclair!' she exclaimed on a gushing note. 'How surprisingly punctual you are!'

Ben was submitted to a thorough once-over in two seconds flat. His gran had said he was dressed too casually, in his black jeans and short-sleeved black and white striped shirt. But Beverly Hollingsworth didn't seem to mind his appearance, not if that gleam in her immaculately made-up eyes was anything to go by.

Ben immediately knew he didn't like her any more in person than he had over the telephone.

'Good evening, Mrs Hollingsworth,' he returned with cool politeness.

'Oh, do call me Beverly. And do come inside out of the heat,' she invited, wrapping both her plump arms around his nearest elbow and drawing him into the vaulted cool of the house.

Ben moved stiffly under her clinging-vine grip, resenting her touch, not to mention the overpoweringly flowery perfume she was wearing. But he allowed himself to be led across the palatial splendour of the foyer, noting the Italian marble floor, the decorative and expensive marble columns, the elegantly curving staircase and the original artwork on the walls.

He was ushered into a living room just as gracious and grand, with everything in shades of cream. He smiled wryly at the thought of Rocky galloping through it with muddy feet. Or a boisterous boy child putting his grubby little hands on one of the pristine sofas.

Clearly this was not a house made for children, or for really living in. It was a showcase for the owner's wealth. Not a *living* room at all. Suddenly he much preferred Gran's old house, with its worn rugs and battered lounge suite.

'Can I get you something to drink, Ben?' Beverly Hollingsworth offered when she at last released him.

'Yes, thanks. I could do with a drink.' What an understatement! He could do with a whole bottle!

'You don't mind me calling you Ben, do you?' She threw a coy smile over her shoulder as she walked towards the bar in the corner.

'Not at all,' Ben said. But he didn't smile back at her. He didn't smile at people he didn't like. 'I'll have whisky. On the rocks.'

'Ah. A real man's drink. Just what I would have expected.'

Ben could not bear it when women old enough to be his mother started coming on to him. He gritted his teeth to stop himself from saying something rude.

'Amber tells me you're a lawyer,' she said as she fixed his drink.

'That's right.'

'You don't look like a lawyer.'

'Really?' Ben declined to ask what he *did* look like. He already knew that in casual clothes he looked like a blue-collar worker, especially with his shirt-collar open and his unruly hair not slicked sleekly back. His dark colouring also meant he suffered from a five o'clock shadow within hours of shaving. In the office he kept an electric shaver in his desk drawer, to help maintain the more civilised façade he was required to adopt for work.

When dressing this afternoon, he'd momentarily regretted not having brought better clothes with him; he'd left his thousand-dollar suits in Sydney. But then he decided Amber's father might respect a more rough and ready man, anyway. Edward Hollingsworth was a self-made millionaire, not a silver spoon. He'd started life as a truck-driver, it was rumoured.

'Not too much ice, I hope?' Beverly simpered as she handed him the whisky.

'It's fine.' Ben was happily putting the glass to his dry lips when he heard a noise behind him.

'Ah, there you are, Amber,' Beverly said in a droll tone before Ben had fully turned round. 'Dressed at long last. Come in, dear. Don't stand there in the doorway like Bette Davis making an entrance.' Her laughter was coldly mocking rather than gently teasing. 'You've no idea how long she's taken to get ready today, Ben. Anyone would think Tom Cruise was coming to dinner.'

The penny dropped. Beverly Hollingsworth did not like her stepdaughter, and was using his presence to try to belittle and embarrass Amber.

And Amber *was* embarrassed. Amazingly. Curiously.

She was also looking incredibly beautiful, in a pale lemon dress vaguely reminiscent of that white ball-gown which had once so aroused him. There was the same flared skirt, a nipped-in waistline, and only the thinnest spaghetti straps holding the tightly fitting bodice up over her still fantastic breasts. She exuded a delicious combination of sensuality and innocence as she walked into the room, her long, straight blonde hair trailing simply down her back and an uncharacteristic flush filling her cheeks as her eyes slid nervously away from his admiring gaze.

Her obvious discomfort sparked the strangest reaction in Ben. Suddenly he felt fiercely protective of her. The urge to smite her wicked witch of a stepmother down where she stood was barely controlled; Ben opted instead for a more subtle counter-attack.

'Well, the end result was certainly worth the effort,' he drawled. 'I have never seen Amber looking more lovely. She looks about eighteen.'

At this, Amber flushed some more, and Ben's stomach flipped right over. When her lovely eyes met his, they searched his face with an odd mixture of apprehension and bewilderment, as though she could not believe he meant his compliment and suspected he would turn enemy at any moment.

'I do hope your stepmother passed on my apologies for yesterday afternoon,' he added sincerely, his eyes not leaving hers.

'Yes, yes she did,' came her oddly hesitant reply.

Ben found he liked this astonishingly uncertain Amber. It made him want to take her in his arms— not to make mad, savage love to her as was usually his secret urge, but just to hold her and comfort her, to repeat his apologies and make her believe that he had never meant to hurt her, had never known he *could* hurt her.

'Amber never did tell me what it was you said to upset her, Ben,' Beverly put in snakily.

'How tactful of her,' he murmured.

Beverly laughed. 'But she called you a bastard all the same.'

Amber's chin lifted, her expression growing proud and aloof in the face of her stepmother's ongoing viciousness. 'True,' she agreed coolly.

This was a side of Amber Ben was well used to, and one which he'd used to despise. But tonight he admired her ability to counter such nastiness with quiet dignity and composure. It was obvious Beverly was jealous of her stepdaughter—an understandable emotion, considering Amber's blinding beauty.

'Amber knows me well,' he concurred with a small smile. 'And she is quite right. My behaviour to her in the past has been most reprehensible. I am quite ashamed of myself and hope that, in time, she will learn to forgive me.'

Beverly looked most put out, and Amber quite confused.

'Really?' Beverly said tartly. 'I can't imagine what you could have done that was so dreadful—unless it was to ignore our darling Amber. She does so hate being ignored, don't you, dear? Still, I can't think of a better evening during which to patch up old differences. I know for a fact that Amber's father would be delighted if you two could become friends. There isn't anything Amber wouldn't do for her father, is there, dear?'

'Not within reason, Beverly,' she replied tautly.

'Under the circumstances, then, I'm sure you won't mind my leaving you to look after Ben while I go and help Edward get ready for dinner.'

Ben watched Amber almost panic as her stepmother swept from the room. But then, just as swiftly, she appeared to gather herself, whirling to set angry eyes upon him.

'Just what are you playing at, Ben Sinclair? All that abject apologising doesn't ring true. Neither do the smarmy compliments. What are you up to? And why did you agree to come here at all? Or can I guess? It wouldn't have anything to do with cold, hard cash, would it? Or is it that you can't resist an opportunity to put the knife into me and twist it?'

Ben sighed. He should have known that things couldn't be smoothed over with Amber as easily as that; he should have known his apology would fall on deaf ears. But he'd had to try.

'Amber, for pity's sake—' he began unhappily.

'For *pity's* sake?' she snapped. 'When did you ever have any pity for me? Or anyone else, for that matter?'

He said nothing for a few seconds. Just stood and stared at her, at her high colour and her shaking shoulders.

'You're right,' he said quietly at last. 'I was a selfish, self-absorbed boy. And I grew into a selfish, self-absorbed man. But I can change, Amber. I *have* changed. You're right when you say I never felt any pity for you in the past. I didn't. I was too busy feeling more basic things than pity.'

He was appalled when tears filled her eyes.

'Dear God, Amber,' he choked out. 'Don't cry...'

'I'm not crying!' she denied, blinking frantically. 'And as for your having changed, I didn't see much change in you yesterday afternoon!'

He finger-combed his wayward waves back from his forehead with both hands. 'You're making me feel rotten.'

'You made *me* feel rotten,' she flung back at him.

'I didn't mean to,' he told her as he shook his head in genuine remorse. 'I don't know why I did what I did. I was wrong.'

That bewilderment was back in her face, plus a touching vulnerability. Obviously she didn't know whether to believe him or not.

But she wanted to. He could see the desperation behind her searching eyes.

'I was an angry young man when I first met you, Amber,' he tried to explain. 'I resented everything, and everyone. I never stopped long enough to know the real you. I thought of you in clichés. Beautiful. Rich. Superior. Sexy. Unattainable...'

She said nothing. Just kept on staring at him.

'I see now I never knew the real you. But I'd like to, Amber. I'd like to very much...'

When he took a step towards her, her hands flung up in renewed panic. 'Don't you dare touch me!'

He hesitated, then decided to ignore her. He put down his drink and came forward, curving gentle hands over her bare shoulders. Her eyes flew to his, as blue and deep as the ocean. His mouth had begun to descend when suddenly she wrenched out of his grip, staggering backwards a few steps.

'Do you honestly think I would let you do that to me again?' she demanded shakily. 'I am not and never have been a slut. Not that you would believe me, despite all that rubbish you just came out with. The only me you've ever wanted to know is the infatuated fool who let you do what you wanted that rotten night. But I'm not some wind-up sex toy which you can use whenever it takes your fancy then toss aside. I'm a flesh and blood person. A human being. I have *feelings*! I can be *hurt*!'

Her tirade over, Amber stood there trembling from head to toe. Ben was more than a little shaken himself. Had he heard wrong when she'd just described herself as an infatuated fool? And why would she be so frightened of his touching her?

Possibilities set Ben's brain ticking over and his heart racing.

Wickedly satisfying scenarios filled his mind, and played perhaps too clearly on his face.

Immediately Amber's top lip curled with open contempt. 'Yes, that look is much more like the Ben I've come to know and despise,' she scorned. 'Please don't bother to hide your true feelings for me in future. And, for pity's sake, don't try to con me with patently false compliments. You're just wasting your breath.

'After all, it's not *me* making the deals for Hollingsworths now. Dad's taken the helm once more. I agreed to be present at this dinner tonight strictly because he asked me to be here, and for no other reason. So don't flatter yourself that it has anything to do with you. Neither does my appearance. I happen to be going out after dinner on a late date.'

This news hit Ben like a physical blow. The image of Amber lying in the arms of another man later that night brought with it a violent jealousy which did not augur well for his mood or manner over dinner.

He reached for the whisky he'd put down earlier and drained the glass with one deep swallow, slamming it back down again on the bar-top.

'How conveniently cheap for your date,' he drawled with savage coldness. 'He doesn't even have to buy you dinner to have you for afters. Who *is* the lucky fellow? A local businessman? Soldier? Sailor? Indian chief? Not telling? Now, why is that, I wonder? Gran said your name wasn't linked with anyone in town at the moment. Which leads me to puzzle over why you might want to keep the identity of your lover a secret.'

Ben was on a roll, the snide words spilling from his mouth like cans from a conveyor belt. 'Ah...now I get the picture. He's married. How very sophisticated of you, Amber. I do hope this country hick husband can live up to your no doubt high standards in the bedding department. Frankly, I have no idea why a woman of your refined tastes has buried herself in this backwater. Surely, after your brilliant marriage to one of the world's most publicised playboys, you find dear old Sunrise Point and its inhabitants a touch boring?'

Ben gained some satisfaction in watching Amber struggle for control. There was a perverse excitement in knowing how much he could still rattle her. This was familiar ground between them, and far less threatening than his earlier moments of vulnerability where she was concerned. For a while there he'd actually begun thinking he'd been totally wrong about her. He'd even wanted to comfort her, *protect* her. She needed about as much protecting as a prickly pear!

Her blue eyes blazed and he could almost see fire smoking from her flared nostrils.

'The only thing I find boring in Sunrise Point,' she scorned, 'is the narrow minds of hypocrites like yourself! I see no reason why I should defend myself to you. Neither will I resort to excuses to refute what Beverly so sweetly put into your mind earlier on. I actually lied about having a later date because I could not bear your smug presumption that I would doll myself up for the likes of you. Believe me when I tell you *this* is not dolled up in my eyes.'

She swept an angry hand down the front of her admittedly simple dress. 'As to your other perennial presumptions about me which are not true—I am not in any way promiscuous. Never have been. I do not have a lover at all at the moment. I have not been with a man since I left my husband three years ago.'

Ben's mouth went dry with her words. She had to be lying. She *had* to be!

She laughed at him. 'I can see by the look on your face that you don't believe me. But what's new? It's always suited you to believe the worst of me,' she spat. 'It justifies your own behaviour that night, which was even more disgusting than mine. Because you were cruel and mean and small-minded, whereas I was merely a foolish teenager who naively didn't know any better. But I'm no longer naive, even though I can still behave a little foolishly, as I did when you kissed me yesterday. And I certainly was *very* foolish earlier this evening when I began to believe you'd changed. But you haven't. You're still cruel and mean and narrow-minded!'

'What's going on here?' came an exasperated growl from the doorway. 'Amber, you're not insulting our dinner guest, are you?'

Ben's eyes snapped round to take in Edward Hollingsworth in a wheelchair, with a smug-faced Beverly standing behind him. She seemed very pleased with this turn of events. Whilst Amber's father's cantankerous comment rankled, Ben found it was his intense dislike for her stepmother which renewed his perverse protectiveness towards Amber.

'Not at all!' he denied jokingly, even while his heart remained in turmoil. 'Amber and I enjoy a little verbal sparring from time to time. We've been doing it since we were kids at school. I tell her how spoiled she is and she tells me how small-minded I am. We enjoy it, don't we, sweetheart?'

Amber didn't answer. His calling her sweetheart had clearly stunned her into silence. It seemed to have similarly affected the couple in the doorway.

Ben decided he might as well be hung for a sheep as a lamb. Aside from wanting to keep that ugly gold-fish look on Beverly Hollingsworth's face, there was no way he could simply walk away from Amber now without finding out the whole potentially appalling truth about her claims of recent celibacy, plus her more astonishing claim of never having been promiscuous. That hardly coincided with what Chris had said about her.

Ben was determined now to find out the whole truth. About her relationship with Chris, her marriage. But most of all about her real feelings for him.

Whatever they were, they were very strong. They *had* to be to have made her this upset with him.

He walked over and curved an intimate arm around her shoulder, squeezing her tightly against his side.

'You're a naughty girl, making them think we don't like each other. Amber and I go back a long way, Mr Hollingsworth. We don't always see eye to eye, especially lately, but we've just cleared the air to a degree, and I would appreciate the opportunity to talk with your daughter further later this evening in private. How about coming for a little drive with me after dinner, Amber?'

She turned her face up to look at him. He could feel her stiffly held muscles, but her eyes were strangely unreadable. Glazed, almost. His own gaze dropped to her slightly parted lips, and the urge to cover them with his own was intense.

'Amber doesn't go for late-night car rides with men, do you, dear?'

Ben would be forever grateful that Beverly chose that moment to speak. For it seemed to galvanise Amber into action, and tip the scales in his favour. Her blue eyes cleared and she gave her stepmother a coldly contemptuous glance.

'Not usually,' she agreed. 'But Ben's different. Ben can be trusted—can't you, darling?'

Ben knew the comment was all sarcasm, and the endearment a double-edged sword, but he liked them all the same. He also enjoyed the effect they had on the wicked witch. Her mouth literally dropped open, then snapped shut in barely held fury. Amber's father merely looked curious, his sharp blue eyes going from his daughter to his guest then back to his daughter again.

He was a big man, Ben noted, and despite not looking all that well, he was still a formidable presence. The sort of man who liked getting his own way, and who would not pull any punches in achieving his goals. He hadn't achieved his ruthless reputation for nothing.

'Well, well, well,' Edward drawled. 'This is a turn-up for the books. Does this sudden mutual admiration society mean you might be more amenable to selling us your land now, Mr Sinclair?'

Ben had almost forgotten about the farm. Not to mention the harassing phone calls. He remembered them now.

'Afraid not,' he returned with deceptive nonchalance. 'The farm belongs to Gran and she doesn't want to sell. Neither will she be frightened off.'

Amber's father stiffened in the wheelchair. 'What do you mean...frightened off?'

'She's been receiving threatening phone calls.'

'Do you know from whom?'

'Not yet. But if I ever find out...'

The two men locked eyes across the room.

'It isn't anyone connected with Hollingsworths,' Edward growled.

'I hope not,' Ben said calmly.

His host scowled. 'Pearl's not going to go to the local paper with this too, is she?'

'I have no idea.'

'There's such a thing as libel and slander, you know.'

'I am acquainted with the terms.'

'Then I suggest you warn your grandmother I will not hesitate to sue if my good name is besmirched again.'

'That's your prerogative.'

Edward Hollingsworth was clearly disgruntled by the exchange. 'You're a cool one, aren't you?'

'Not always.' He wasn't feeling at all cool with his arm around Amber and her side pressed firmly against his.

'So there's no point my making a new pitch to you for the farm over a glass of wine?' her father asked testily. 'No point my offering more money?'

'No point at all.'

'But you're still going to eat my dinner and take out my daughter?' he grumped.

Ben smiled. 'With your permission, sir.'

'Huh! Amber never asks my permission before she does things these days. But her happiness is very important to me. Will going out with this impertinent young man make you happy, daughter?'

'Probably not.'

'But you'll go anyway?'

'If Ben insists.'

Ben raised his eyebrows, then glanced down at the amazingly cool-sounding Amber.

She hadn't moved an inch since he'd put his arm around her. Was she as aroused as he was by their closeness to each other?

He recalled how she'd once responded quite blindly to macho assertiveness. Clearly she'd liked his taking charge that night, liked his masterful display.

Or was it that she'd been so infatuated with him back then that he could have acted any way and succeeded in seducing her?

God knew what the truth was. You could never be sure with Amber. All he knew was that he wanted her now more than ever. Three years without a man, he kept thinking. If that was true he'd like the chance to redress that situation.

He tried to look as cool as she was acting when he gazed down at her. But he had a feeling something of his inner hunger and intensity must have communicated itself to her, drawing her eyes up to his like a magnet. With her chin tipped up like that only inches separated their faces, and their mouths. He almost kissed her then and there, almost crashed his mouth down on hers in a passionate obliteration of this painfully casual façade he was hiding behind.

But he feared that to do so might spoil whatever chance he had with her. Somehow he managed to find a carefree and hopefully disarming smile.

'Oh, I insist, Amber,' he said with a low laugh. 'I insist.'

CHAPTER EIGHT

AMBER made her decision somewhere between dessert and coffee. During the first two courses of the meal a mental war had raged in her mind, where every survival instinct she owned screamed at her not to go with Ben later. He could definitely *not* be trusted. Experience told her he didn't want to *talk* at all! He just wanted to take up where he'd left off ten years earlier.

His desire for her had been a palpable thing back in the living room. She'd been petrified at one stage that he'd been going to kiss her right there, in front of her father. Lord knew what she would have done if he had. Melted right into him, she supposed. She'd begun to burn for him from the moment he'd put his damned arm around her.

No, that was a lie. The burning had begun the moment she'd seen him standing there, idly sipping a drink, yet looking incredibly sexy and dynamic against the living room's anaemic decor.

Ben had resembled a big black jungle cat, pretending to be tamed for a while, sleek of line and deceptively civilised on the outside. But the second he'd turned and set those hungry black eyes on her, Amber had glimpsed the predatory beast beneath. The hunter. Ben might have acquired a veneer of sophistication with the years—he could even ape sympathy and sensitivity when it suited him, it seemed—but deep down he was still a wild animal who lived by basic instincts alone.

Sex was as elemental to him as eating and sleeping. And he wanted to have sex with her. Uninterrupted and ultimately satisfying sex.

She'd been wrong about his coming here tonight to get a better offer for his gran's farm. He'd come here for one thing and one thing only.

Once Amber had accepted that—plus her own reaction to this realisation—she stopped fighting herself. For the truth was she wanted to have sex with Ben as much as he wanted to have sex with her.

Since leaving Chad, Amber had endeavoured to be more honest with herself all round. Hypocrisy of emotion had for too long fashioned her actions. She'd told her husband for years that she loved him, because the alternative had been too scary to contemplate.

Now, she looked at Ben across the dinner table and simply refused to allow the inevitability of their becoming lovers frighten her any more.

What was the worst that could happen? she asked herself as she lifted her coffee cup to her lips. That she fall in love with him?

Can't happen, Amber, a little voice whispered in her head. 'Cause you already are…

Amber's sharp intake of breath had Ben taking his own coffee cup away from his lips and staring over the rim at her. Not his first stare at her over dinner, but definitely his most thoughtful.

'Coffee too hot?' he asked.

'A little,' came her taut reply.

But it wasn't the coffee which was hot all of a sudden. Amber rattled the cup back into her saucer and tried to swallow the huge lump in her throat.

She concentrated her gaze on the back of Ben's hand, rather than on those far too sharp eyes of his. But soon she found herself staring at the black hairs curling against his olive skin and wondering what he would look like naked. It was not the most cooling or calming thought.

'That was an excellent dinner, Mrs Hollingsworth,' Ben was saying while Amber tried to pull herself together. 'And excellent wine, Edward. I would have liked to sample some more of it, but I'm careful of my drinking when I drive.'

'Sensible,' Edward muttered from where he was slumping a little sidewards in his wheelchair. 'Sorry to bring the evening to an abrupt end, folks, but I find sitting up straight for this length of time quite exhausting.'

The antique grandfather clock in the corner had just donged ten.

'I've certainly enjoyed your company, Ben,' Amber's father continued. 'You're not at all as I pictured after my daughter's description. Amber, you must invite him here more often. As for your grandmother's land, I think Hollingsworths will have to find another solution to their car park problem.'

Amber frowned at her father. She could not believe he was giving up so quickly. He hadn't even tried to get Ben to persuade his grandmother to sell. That wasn't like her father at all!

He seemed to read her mind. 'You don't have to look at me like that, daughter dear. This shopping mall was your idea in the first place. I hereby place the problem back in your no doubt more capable hands. From what I can see, you'll have more success talking Ben here into something than I would. Isn't that right, Ben?'

Ben's dark eyes glittered while one eyebrow lifted. 'Undoubtedly so,' he drawled. 'I am putty in her hands.'

Amber smouldered with bitter resentment at his absolute untruth. It was *she* who was the putty in *his* hands. And he knew it, the devious devil!

'You'd better get me to my room, Bev,' her father grated out through obviously gritted teeth. 'Unfortunately, I must have drunk your share of the wine, Ben. At least, that's what my bladder is telling me.'

Amber realised she'd drunk quite a few glasses of wine over dinner as well. Her head was spinning a little and there was a fizzy feeling running all through her body.

An excess of alcohol always had a tendency to make her recklessly uncaring. Chad had introduced her to drinking on their honeymoon. He would have liked to introduce her to several other drugs as well, but luckily she'd resisted that pressure. Still, she'd become somewhat of a tippler during her marriage, especially in the evening before going to bed. It had been the only way she could face Chad's never-ending attentions.

But she didn't think being recklessly uncaring was too good an idea if she was to go for a drive with Ben and try to resist what he had in mind. For she did have to resist any physical overtures now, didn't she? Now that she knew she loved him.

He claimed he'd changed and that he wanted a new relationship with her. But that didn't tally with the way he had looked at her when she'd claimed relative innocence earlier in the evening. His face had betrayed a cynical disbelief.

No, his opinion of her remained unchanged. He still believed she opened her legs at the drop of a hat.

How could she, knowing that, give her body to him a second time to use without any depth of caring or tenderness? It was an impossible and distasteful situation and one which pride alone would not allow.

'Are you ready to go, Amber?' Ben asked, once her father and stepmother had departed.

Her eyes lifted back to his, painful with their discoveries and their decision making. No, she could not bear to do that to herself, she reinforced.

But Amber was still fiercely curious over what he had to say for himself. And she was still, she supposed, willing to try to persuade him to get his gran to sell that land. If there was even a small chance of either of those things happening, then she simply had to go with him. But not blindly. And not naively.

'I will come—on one condition,' she stated firmly, then immediately wished she hadn't phrased it quite that way.

To give Ben credit, he didn't appear to notice the unfortunate *double entendre*. 'And what's that?'

'You will keep your hands to yourself,' she said, and glared daggers at him. 'You said you wanted to talk. Well, that's the deal. Just talk. Take it or leave it.'

'All right,' he said crisply. 'I'll take it.'

She frowned. 'Now, why do I think that was too easy?'

'Because you don't trust me?' he suggested.

She laughed.

'Or is it that you don't trust yourself?' he added drily.

She pulled a face at him and stood up, holding onto the back of the chair so that she didn't sway from her suddenly light head. 'Don't flatter yourself, Ben. You're not that irresistible.'

'Oh, do shut up, Amber, and come along. Or were those words about my keeping my hands off just so much rhetoric? Is it that you really want me to drag you out of here and do what I did ten years ago?'

Amber could not believe the burst of erotic excitement which flooded her at his hot, angry words.

'You wouldn't dare!'

'You're wrong, Amber. I would dare. But I won't do it because there is more at stake here than simply screwing you. Look, I'm sick to death of the way we act whenever we're together. It's beneath us, and it's not damned well necessary. We're not over-sexed adolescents any more. We're adults, and as such should be able to control our bodies—and our tongues. I want to talk to you like an adult. I want to communicate properly. I want to know all there is to know about you. And I don't mean biblically speaking!

'So, what do you say?' he added after a few seconds' electric silence.

'What do I say?' she echoed blankly, her tongue feeling thick and furry in her mouth.

He smiled at her as he had never smiled before. It was sweet and warm and funny, and it curled around her heart. 'Give it to me. I can take it.'

True, she thought. He'd taken everything she'd ever dished out to him. Taken it and come back for more.

Why would he have done that, if he didn't care about her?

Her stomach went into instant knots. Her heart thudded. Her head spun. 'I say...I'll have to go to the bathroom first!'

Ben blinked, then laughed. 'Trust you to cut to essentials. But you're quite right. I could do with a trip to the loo myself. Which way to the gents?'

Amber was amazed at how a simple conversation

about toilets could defuse the excruciating tension and emotion which had been building in her body.

'This way,' she told him, and led him along the hallway to the downstairs powder room. 'That one can be yours,' she said, pointing. 'I'll duck upstairs to my own private domain and meet you at the front door in a couple of minutes.'

She was very relieved to be able to dash upstairs and give herself a few private moments to collect herself and try to put what had just happened into perspective.

Ben was right when he said they were adults now. *He* certainly was. And a lawyer to boot, she told herself as she brushed her hair and refreshed her lipstick. A practised orator. A persuader. And, possibly, a deceiver.

Don't be so ready to be taken in by a few impassioned words and a nice smile, she told herself. The man has never treated you with respect before. Why now? Why tonight?

Cynicism suggested he might still be angling for an exorbitant price for his grandmother's farm, with a little vengeful nookie into the bargain.

Watch yourself, Amber. Leopards don't change their spots.

Amber tried to catch herself in time, but she had automatically sprayed herself with perfume as part of her freshening up routine without thinking. She'd worn this particular perfume on and off since she was sixteen, her father having given her her first big bottle for her sixteenth birthday. It had been her mother's favourite and was called Boudoir. It was a very subtle, musky scent. Not strong at all. Amber found it pleasant without being overpowering. But most men seemed to really like it. Chris had claimed it drove him mad. Chad had liked her to spray it all over her body.

Amber never wore it to work. She had deliberately not worn it for dinner tonight. For perfectly obvious reasons, she'd been afraid to.

She now fervently wished she could wash it off. Unfortunately, because of the perfume's relatively weak smell, she'd got into the habit of always spraying from the bottle liberally. Now it clung to her hair, her neck, her clothes. She contemplated changing, but that would look odd. It might even be a more provocative move than applying the perfume in the first place.

No. She would just have to brazen out the situation.

'Damn,' she muttered as she left her bedroom. Why was she always having to play a part with Ben? Why could she never be herself?

She walked with unhurried movements down the stairs, schooling her face as she went into an expression of coolly confident composure.

She feared she was not entirely successful.

CHAPTER NINE

BEN sucked in a deep breath as he watched Amber descend the staircase. Her step was slow, her blue eyes chillingly wary upon him once more.

His exasperation was acute. Even that short time apart had done irreparable damage. She was back to distrusting him, doubting him.

Damn and blast! He ground his teeth in frustration. One step forward and two steps backwards. That was how it would always be with her.

But as she drew nearer, and lifted her chin in that proud way she had when defying him, he caught a whiff of perfume which he could have sworn was the same one she'd worn that night all those years ago. It was a lightly exotic smell, which suggested rather than swamped. The effect was teasing and elusive. Ben found it incredibly arousing.

He frowned. She hadn't been wearing that perfume at dinner. But she was wearing it now.

Why?

In view of everything which had transpired between them, there seemed only one answer. And, whilst he found this reason exciting, it wasn't one he especially liked.

* * *

Amber watched for his face to show a mocking recognition of her potentially telling use of perfume. She *did* see a momentary clouding in his eyes, which might have heralded his noticing, followed by one of those darkly brooding expressions which could mean just about anything.

'Where are you taking me for this in-depth discussion?' she asked, her sharp tone reflecting her growing unease.

Ben shrugged. 'How about the look-out on the point? That's always a popular destination for a Saturday evening drive.'

It was also a type of lovers' lane, where couples steamed up the windows of their cars.

'I don't think so,' she said snippily, and gave him a reproachful look.

'Then you suggest somewhere,' he countered.

Amber thought of the cottage, where she'd spent some hours today, seeing what was needed before she could move in. It was probably the ideal place, if she could be sure Ben wouldn't pounce. But she wasn't at all confident of his intentions as yet.

'Let's just drive down to the beach and walk along the sand. It's warm enough.'

'Which beach? North or South?'

North Sunrise Beach was the longest and the quietest. But it was invariably besieged by teenage lovers on a Saturday night because of its high sandhills and its coverage of thick vegetation. South Sunrise was smaller, with fewer hide-aways.

'South, I think,' she said.

'South, it is,' he agreed without hesitation, putting her mind at rest a bit.

'You go on down to the car,' she suggested. 'I want to say goodnight to Dad. I'll join you in a minute or two.'

'Fair enough.'

Amber found her father already in bed and Beverly nowhere in sight. She wondered if her stepmother was lurking around the house somewhere, trying to over-hear what went on between herself and Ben. She wouldn't put it past her.

'Well, daughter?' her father queried when she went in. 'What have you got to say for yourself?'

'About what?'

'About you and Ben Sinclair.'

'What about me and Ben Sinclair?'

He laughed. 'So that's the way you're going to play it. Fair enough. You're old enough to be entitled to your privacy.'

'I'm also old enough to have a place of my own.'

He scowled at her. 'Meaning?'

'Meaning I'm going to move out, Dad. I really ap-preciate all you've done for me since my divorce from Chad, but it's time I stood on my own two feet.'

He nodded slowly, recognising the sense of what she was saying while obviously regretting that he would not have her under his roof any more. Amber felt a tug of guilt at leaving him when he was still not a hundred percent. She contemplated telling him of her problems with Beverly but decided that it would not serve any purpose, would only upset him.

'Do you have somewhere in mind?' he asked. 'You're not going to move away altogether, are you?'

'No, never. I like living in Sunrise. And I like working for you. There's this cottage the company bought recently up on Oceanview Hill which I especially like. I don't expect you to give it to me, of course. I'll buy it with some of my own money.'

'I didn't know you had any. Didn't you waive any alimony in exchange for an uncontested divorce?'

'In the main. Not that Chad had all that much actual cash left at the time of our divorce. He *did* give me a lot of jewellery during those six years, however. Some of which I've sold.'

Actually, she'd sold the lot, not being able to bear to wear any of it any more. It had felt like prices paid for services rendered. The same with all the designer evening gowns her husband had liked her to wear. They'd gone to a good second-hand clothing store. None of them had been to her taste, anyway. Chad had liked his prized possession of a wife to look sexy all the time, with clinging clothes and showy jewellery. Yet at the same time he'd been fiercely jealous of any man who had paid her any attention.

She shuddered to think of all she'd put up with during her marriage. She hadn't got out of that ghastly situation one minute too soon.

'And don't forget, Dad,' she swept on, before too many more memories crowded in, 'you've been paying me a very generous salary for three years now, from which I've saved heaps.'

'You? Saved money? That's a new one. Before you left home you went through your allowance like it was water!'

'Yes, well, I was a very silly young girl back then. Now I'm hopefully a more mature adult who values money and despises waste. Besides, what have I had to spend any money on lately? You let me live here free of charge and my needs have been pretty basic. Look, Ben's waiting for me in the car, so I'd better go.' She bent to give him a peck on the cheek.

He was frowning when she lifted her head. 'That's your mother's perfume you're wearing.'

'Yes, that's right.'

'Beautiful woman, your mother,' he murmured thoughtfully. 'You're just like her.'

'So you've told me.'

'Your mother could also be very naughty sometimes.' He frowned at her some more. 'You're not just playing with Ben, are you, Amber? I mean, you wouldn't do anything you shouldn't do just to get him to sell you that land, would you?'

Amber laughed. 'No woman plays with Ben, Dad. Not unless she wants to get burnt.'

'Is that what happened to you once? Did he burn you?'

'Sort of. But I think he came away a little singed himself. Now, do stop being a nosy father. I'll let you know if and when there's anything worthwhile to tell you about Ben and myself.'

'Huh! You never really tell me anything. You never really tell *anybody* anything. Beverly's been most put out that you've never confided in her in a woman to woman fashion.'

'I guess I'm just not much of a confider all round,' she said drily, not wanting to get into a discussion about her shortcomings where Beverly was concerned. 'Night, Dad. Sleep tight.'

She fled the room before he could churn her up any further. Not only had he brought up her nightmare of a marriage and her past history with Ben, but he'd even made her feel oddly guilty over her treatment of Beverly. Okay, so she'd never confided in her step-mother. But Beverly was hardly a sympathetic listener. Anyway, her father was right. She'd never confided in anyone—because he'd been too damned busy to talk to her since her mother had died.

It was too late for her to change now. Too late for her to become one of those women who chatted easily with other women, who gossiped and forged friendships through shared confidences.

She hurried down the front steps and climbed into the passenger seat of Ben's car, apologising profusely to Ben over how long she'd been.

'It's okay,' Ben said, although there was an edge in his voice. 'I've waited ten years for this night. A few minutes more won't make any difference.'

Her head whipped round to stare at him. 'What do

you mean by that?' she asked, dry-mouthed, as he drove off down the steep driveway and onto the main road.

'You know damned well what I mean,' he ground out.

'You…you promised you wouldn't touch me.'

'That was before you came back downstairs, wearing that perfume.'

So he *had* noticed!

'Was I wrong in assuming that meant you'd changed your mind on that score?'

'You certainly were! If that's what you think then you can turn round right now and take me back home! I—'

'Okay, okay—cool it! I'll be a good boy. Besides, I wasn't actually talking about sex when I said I'd waited ten years. Although I have to confess sex is never far from my mind where you're concerned,' he added ruefully. 'I was talking about the opportunity to have things out between us, to stop all the garbage and just be honest. A sort of truth game.'

'Are lawyers acquainted with the truth?' she asked tartly.

He laughed. 'More than most people, since we try to get around it so often.'

Amber frowned at him, realising she knew nothing about his professional or private life these days, except what little she'd gleaned from his gran over one miserable cup of tea.

'And what kind of look is that?' Ben challenged,

without even glancing her way. She wondered if he had eyes in the side of his head.

'I was thinking how little I really know about you.'

'That's exactly what I'm talking about, Amber. We've never stopped long enough to get to know each other properly, to see beyond our initial adolescent opinions. I'd like to try to remedy that.'

'Why bother at this late stage? From what I gathered, you're not far off getting married to some girl back in Sydney.'

His sidewards glare was savage. 'Who, in God's name, told you that?'

'Your gran.'

'Well, she was wrong,' he growled, and Amber's heart leapt.

'You're not getting married?'

'No.'

'Or living with anyone?'

'Good God, no.'

'Why do you say it like that?'

'Because I couldn't think of anything worse than sharing my life with a woman unless I was simply crazy about her. I'm far too selfish to tolerate the compromises I would have to make.'

'I see.'

'Do you, Amber?' he remarked drily.

'Probably not.'

They both fell silent for a while. Amber turned her head to stare rather blankly through the open passenger window. The road they were travelling along skirted the edge of town, winding around the base of the hills which surrounded Sunrise on three sides. They eventually came to a huge roundabout which had multiple exits. North led towards Brisbane. South went to Sydney. West took you into the town centre and east to the beaches.

Ben angled his car round to Beachside Drive, which was a very quiet road with no houses, just bush on either side. Amber lowered the window and leant back in the seat with a sigh. A lovely sea breeze ruffled her hair and the tang of sea salt filled her nostrils.

'What kind of a lawyer are you, Ben?' she asked as the car sped smoothly towards the sea. 'Do you represent people in court?'

'No. I'm an expert in contracts and corporate take-over procedures. I do sometimes help prepare court cases. Not criminal cases, though. Compensation cases. We have a team of QCs who do the actual court work.'

'You don't want to become a QC yourself?'

'And wear that stupid gown and wig? Hell, no.'

'Do you like being a lawyer?'

'Do you want the truth?'

'That's the point of this drive, isn't it?'

'Touché. I guess it's always easier to demand the truth from others than to confess all yourself.'

Amber could not agree more.

'I don't know if it's my profession exactly I'm dissatisfied with,' he admitted. 'All I know is that I'm not enjoying my life in Sydney as much as I should be. Strange, really. I always believed I was a city boy at heart. During the three years I lived and went to school here I couldn't wait to get back to Sydney. I wanted all that being successful in the city could give me. And I *have* got all that now...to a degree.'

'And it hasn't made you happy?'

He slanted her a wry look. 'No, Amber, it hasn't. What about you?'

'Me? What about me?'

'Are you happy?'

'Happy?' she echoed, immediately shrinking back from exposing her inner self, retreating behind safe generalities. 'Happiness is an elusive concept. I guess I'm as happy as most people.'

'You've already forgotten the game, Amber,' he reproached, and swung the car into a small parking bay which faced the beach and the ocean. 'But I expected as much. You're like me. You have to be forced to face the truth. You don't embrace it willingly. But that's all right. I understand where you're coming from since I'm the same, most of the time. But not tonight. Tonight is strictly for the truth, the whole truth and nothing but the truth.'

'So help me God?' she scoffed lightly, but inside she was afraid—afraid of the truth, afraid of him.

He smiled a small ironic smile. 'I could certainly do with a little help tonight, that's for sure. Come on,' he invited as he switched off the engine, 'let's walk.'

He was out of the car before she could say Jack Robinson. Amber hesitated, despite this having been her suggestion. She recalled what had happened the last time she went outside with Ben on her own. But she supposed sitting in a car alone with him was no more secure. Sighing, she climbed out. It was quite breezy outside, but not cold. Her hair whipped out behind her as she walked towards where Ben was holding his hands out to her.

Again, she hesitated. He shrugged, his hands dropping back to his sides. He slid them into the pockets of his jeans and turned to stride towards the stretch of sand which separated them from the water's edge.

Amber groaned to herself as she watched him go, then hurried after him.

'Stop,' she called out when she found it impossible to walk on the sand in her high heels.

He stopped and waited while she slipped the shoes off her feet. Even in bare feet, the sand oozed between her toes as she walked, making it still difficult.

'Let's go closer to the water,' she suggested, 'where the sand is harder.'

They finally walked along side by side, her stride as long and easy as his.

'Go on, then,' he said. 'Tell me. Are you happy?'

Amber toyed with the idea of lying, then decided to hell with it. 'I've had moments of pleasure and personal satisfaction, especially this past year. But I'm not sure I've ever been really happy.'

'You must have been happy as a kid. Jeez, Amber, you had everything!'

She shook her head. 'Materially speaking, maybe,

but I was wretchedly lonely. I ached for someone to lavish real love and attention on me, but it never happened. After my mother died, my father worked twenty-hour days and never had time for me. The people he hired to look after me before and after school didn't give a damn about me.'

Ben pretended to play the violin, and Amber hit him a glancing blow on his arm with one of her sandals.

'Hey, that hurt!' he protested.

'Rubbish!'

'Do it again and I'll put you over my knee,' he warned.

'You and what army?'

He stopped, and for a split second Amber thought he was going to do just that.

'Easily said when you already have my promise not to touch you,' he growled. 'But we're getting off the point of this discussion—which is about present happiness, not the past. If you think I'm going to believe that you had it tough as a child, Amber, then forget it. You don't know what having it tough is!'

'I *was* insufferably spoiled back then,' she agreed. 'But I did suffer, Ben. I know you don't believe me but it's true.'

'Huh! Well, if you did, it wasn't from loneliness. You had more friends—*and* boyfriends—than I could poke a stick at.'

'My money bought me a type of friend, and my looks attracted the boys. But the girls I wanted to like me wouldn't ever let me into their groups. And the boys only ever wanted one thing. Which made me even more determined not to give it to them,' she added ruefully.

'Till Chris came along.'

Amber was taken aback for a second, till she realised that of course Ben believed she'd slept with Chris. She'd finally worked *that* out a long time ago. She wondered if there was any point in clinging to her story that she'd been a virgin before their graduation night.

She glanced up into Ben's handsome face and searched his dark eyes.

'What?' he said, frowning.

'You said you wanted the truth tonight, Ben. Well, I have something to tell you, but I'm reluctant to because I'm afraid you won't believe me. Yet I have no reason to lie. Perhaps if you could remember that...'

His smile was wry. 'I'd believe just about anything about you, Amber. Don't you know that? Give it to me straight. I can take it.'

'Very well. Chris and I *never* had sex. Not before the ball, or that night, or afterwards. His considerable ego was bruised by my going outside with you, and then I broke up with him later that week. He said what he said about me out of revenge. He lied, Ben. I was a virgin before that night. I swear it.'

Amber expected to see automatic disbelief on Ben's face. After all, Chris had been very vocal and explicit over her easy virtue. It was as well the things he'd said she'd done with him had not reached her father's ears.

On top of that there was the way she'd acted with Ben that night. She could hardly blame him for thinking her cheap and easy. *And* experienced. Any male who knew anything at all about sex would have concluded she'd been down that road a hundred times before. The act of penetration itself had been achieved so easily and painlessly, and she herself had been so...responsive. Ben must have jumped to the conclusion that she was a real raver.

So, yes, she'd expected him to be sceptical at this unexpected revelation. What Amber hadn't expected to see in his eyes was emotional turmoil. And pain. He just stood there, staring down at her, not saying a word but looking at her with such distress that in the end she dropped both her sandals onto the wet sand and lifted her hands to cradle his strained face.

'Ben, darling,' she said without thinking, her only wish to comfort him. 'You couldn't have known. I understand that. Don't be upset. I just wanted you to know, that's all. You said you wanted to clear the air. You said you wanted the truth. Well, that's the truth. Honest.'

CHAPTER TEN

BEN had rarely been so totally at a loss in life as he was at that moment. No words came to his rescue. His mouth was bone-dry. A wild rush of emotion had filled his heart—none of which was soothing.

There was no denying Amber was telling him the truth. For why *would* she lie at this stage? He could not even cling to this wild possibility of her lying and thereby save his sanity.

No. She was telling the truth. She'd been a virgin that night. He'd been her first lover, as he'd once fantasised. She must have been so turned on by him, so aroused, that she'd acted totally out of character and lost control. Her body had welcomed him with a passion which had transcended her lack of experience. For once she hadn't been able to hide behind that cool façade which had become her trademark. He'd had the power and the opportunity to win her that night, to win her heart as well as her body.

And he'd ruined it, spoiled everything, because that was the kind of dummy he'd been back then. A distrustful, disbelieving, disagreeable dummy!

A crippling dismay over what might have been flooded Ben. He saw the last ten years flash by, with all its superficial successes. Whatever he'd achieved in his professional life melted away to nothing in the face of the utter personal waste he'd set in place that night of graduation.

Because he'd wanted Amber more than he'd ever wanted money or success. He still did.

Her hands around his face finally registered, as did the 'darling' she'd just called him, plus the astonishing way she was acting towards him. With the deepest of concerns and the tenderest of touches. She might not love him as he loved her, but she did care. And she was still sexually attracted to him.

Yes. Maybe there *was* still a chance for him.

Ben's dismay was immediately obliterated by a wave of ruthless resolve. He might have wasted the last ten years but he would not waste another moment. His heart began to race as his hands came up to cover hers. He lifted her hands from his cheeks and linked them around his neck.

His heart began to pound harder when she made no attempt to remove her arms. His own slid around her narrow waist till his fingers and palms were caressing the small of her back. When her thumbnails dug parallel paths into his hair, an erotic ripple raced down Ben's spine, making him wonder momentarily who was about to make love to whom.

It crossed his mind again that this was what she'd wanted all along. The promise she'd extracted from him not to touch her had been a clever ruse packed with reverse psychology.

It bothered him that she might be so devious. But

her motives were as nothing compared to what he was feeling at that moment. A fierce desire was roaring along his veins, heating his blood and his flesh. He ached to yank her hard against him, to press himself into the soft swell of her stomach.

But he didn't want to ruin his chances a second time with the wrong words or actions. He was going to be more patient this time.

She glanced downwards for some reason, breaking eye contact. Maybe she was just looking for her sandals on the sand. It seemed to Ben, however, that she was staring at the bare inches which separated their bodies from total contact. He felt her stiffen all of a sudden, felt her fear.

He recalled how he'd once got past her better judgement by being masterful. He understood she would resent any real aggression here tonight, but, still, she needed encouragement—and direction.

'Amber, look at me,' was all he said. But firmly, strongly.

Moonlight played on her face as she slowly tipped it up towards his, dancing across her high cheekbones and across the point of her pert nose. It was an intriguingly beautiful face, a fascinating mixture of sensuality and innocence. She hadn't aged at all in those ten years; her fair skin was unlined, her eyes sparklingly clear, that mouth as lush and full as ever.

'Yes?' she asked, her lips staying parted with soft invitation.

Nothing of her was touching him except her arms.

But her body beckoned, as did the perfume wafting from every inch of her. He wanted to drink it in, drink *her* in. His head began to bend and he told himself nothing would stop him this time.

Amber knew he was going to kiss her.

Too late to run. Too late to do anything but let him. She'd just called him 'darling', after all; she'd just told him in so many words how much he meant to her.

It was a surprisingly gentle kiss. Long and slow and tender, his mouth moving lightly over hers. Yet, for all their softness, Ben's lips evoked a strong impression of possession. A branding, so to speak. You are *my* woman, they seemed to be saying.

Amber gradually grew light-headed—maybe with her lack of air. By the time his tongue slid deep into her mouth she was clinging to him, her head tipped back, her long hair falling away from her back, her breasts pressed flat against his chest. She was offering him more than her mouth. She was offering him herself.

And he took her up on the offer, his arms winding her even tighter against him, his hands tangling in her hair. His kisses turned hungry, as did his hands. One wound her hair around and around, then tugged it back to keep her back arched against him. The other followed the curve of her spine till it was cupping her bottom and moulding her abdomen to his. She could feel his erection through their clothes, feel his need.

She could feel her own need as well, hot and wild within her. She wanted him inside her, filling her, taking her to that place she'd never been to before.

She moaned against his mouth.

A rogue wave crashing round their ankles didn't dampen their desire at all. Ben merely swept her up into his arms and carried her back across the sand towards the car. Dazedly, she made no protest, uncaring that her expensive shoes were probably at that moment washing out to sea.

He placed her carefully on the back seat before climbing in behind the wheel and reversing out from the potentially public car park. He drove to a smaller and more private lay-by further down the beach. It was edged with low thick trees under which Ben eased the car.

As the black bonnet merged into the shadows Amber began to shiver uncontrollably. Not with cold—it was a very warm night—but with a feverish excitement. There was no longer any question of stopping. She loved Ben, and she believed now that he loved her back. She'd waited ten years for this moment and would not tolerate any further interruption to their being one—as they had always been meant to be!

By the time Ben opened the back door she was sitting up. When he climbed in beside her and shut the door, she immediately reached for him.

But he pulled back from her eager embrace, dark eyes troubled. 'Amber, I—'

'No, don't,' she broke in, hushing him further by placing her fingers against his mouth. 'Don't speak. Don't think. Don't worry.'

She took his right hand and slid it up her leg under her skirt, leaving it on the soft swell of her inner thigh, barely inches from where she was literally burning for his touch. 'This was always meant to be, Ben,' she told him breathlessly. 'You. Me. Together like this.'

She cupped his face and stared deep into his eyes. 'No more talk,' she insisted huskily. 'Nothing but this.' And she kissed him passionately, sending her tongue deep into his mouth, its movement echoing what she wanted his body to do to hers.

He kissed her back just as fiercely and suddenly. Her feelings had little to do with sentiment and everything to do with sex. Raw and primitive and naked.

When Ben's hand crossed those final few inches and began stroking her through her panties, Amber thought she was going to explode. She gasped, then moaned at the wet heat of her desire.

His ripping her underwear off startled her but did not shock her. For, in a weird kind of way, this was what she wanted. For Ben to be as out of control as she had once been in *his* arms. Yet, when his fingers returned to her now naked flesh, it was she who was soon beside herself. She writhed against his knowing touch, her knees falling evocatively apart as he explored her with devastating intimacy. He had her pressed up against the back seat and was kissing her at the same time, taking control of every part of their lovemaking. His tongue was surging into her in tandem with his fingers.

She came with exquisite physical pleasure, but also with a degree of emotional dismay. For this was not what she'd dreamt about all these years. She'd wanted him inside her when she came, wanted him to feel her body pulsating around him, her long-imagined ecstasy bringing him to ecstasy as well.

Her madly racing heartbeat had barely calmed when Ben stopped kissing her and turned his attention to the rest of her clothes. Her heart skipped a beat each time he slipped one of the thin straps off her shoulders, then lurched when, without undoing the zipper, he peeled the figure-hugging bodice of her dress down to her waist.

Amber could feel her breasts straining against the strapless bra she was wearing. The half-cups of white satin were highly inadequate to house her swollen curves. Her ragged breathing had them bulging out everywhere, her hardened nipples barely covered.

She bent forward slightly to help him undo the restraining garment, a shuddering sigh escaping her lips when the clasp was released. She felt a rush of adrenalin at knowing her breasts would shortly be naked to his eyes. And his touch. She'd thought about his touching her bare breasts often as she lay in bed in the dead of night, thought of him licking them and sucking them.

Her stomach curled over at the thought that all her fantasies might soon come true.

'Amber,' he said, breaking the mood of the moment for a second.

She looked at him rather blankly.

'Let go,' he ordered.

Amber blinked before realising she was holding on to the front of her bra like grim death.

'Oh,' she said, flushing wildly as she let him take the bra and toss it aside.

When Ben returned his attention to her upper body, naked now to the waist, Amber suddenly wished it were pitch-black in the car. For some reason she felt acutely embarrassed, and even more naked than if she'd been sitting there totally nude.

Unfortunately it wasn't pitch-black. A certain amount of moonlight was filtering through the windows and Amber's eyes had long grown used to the dimness. No doubt Ben's had as well. Since she could see *him* perfectly well, it was only logical that she was similarly exposed to his sight.

Amber's embarrassment—or was it excitement?—increased as she just sat there while Ben seemed to be inspecting her at great length, his hands following his travelling gaze, lightly tracing over her shoulders then smoothing down her arms before moving over to her ribs. He drew invisible lines along each one, making her skin quiver and her stomach tighten. By the time he moved up to her breasts she was almost feeling sick with tension. Even then he didn't touch them as she'd thought—and hoped—he might. At first he just caressed their sides with soft, sweeping strokes, then he cupped the heavy curves beneath her nipples, his thumbs going close to but never quite touching the expectant peaks.

Amber found that soon she was literally holding her breath. When he finally did draw near to a nipple, it was with a single teasing fingertip, moving it in tantalising circles around each of her tiny pink areolae in turn, but still without actually touching either of the highly sensitive centres.

They had responded nevertheless during this excitingly erotic torture, standing erect like twin sentinels, stiff and tall and tautly swollen. Amber's face had grown very hot as well. Her head was spinning.

'Just do it, for God's sake,' she groaned at last, her head flopping back against the seat, her eyes squeezed shut as she thrust her breasts eagerly forward.

'Just do what?'

Her eyes shot open at the coolly delivered words.

Ben was staring at her suddenly as though he didn't like her very much. His eyes had that angry, resentful look he'd used to give her at school.

'I... I...' Her voice died. Because she could not say aloud what she wanted him to do without it sounding bad.

'Never mind, Amber,' he muttered. 'I know what you want.' And he bent to start tonguing each nipple in turn, taking her breath away along with any protest.

But the pleasure did not entirely blind her to reality, and Amber worried that Ben had the wrong idea about what was happening here between them, and what she felt for him.

She was considering saying something when he changed from licking to sucking, and everything inside her crunched down hard. Dear God, she could hardly think straight any more, her hands flopping back on the leather seat, her eyes closing on a sensual shudder. But it was just so delicious, his mouth wet and hot upon her, drawing feelings from her breasts and from deep inside as he suckled on her like a baby.

But he was not a baby, she conceded dazedly. He was a man. A man who had always been able to do this to her. Turn her inside out.

Maybe it was *she* who was wrong. Maybe it *was* only sex which bound them. The physical feelings he was evoking in her were beginning to override everything. All of a sudden it didn't seem to matter whether he loved her or not, as long as he *made* love to her. The tension building within her body was excruciating, and impossible to ignore. She simply had to have him. And soon.

'Don't stop,' she protested shakily when he suddenly abandoned her breasts.

He said nothing, just reached to lock all the car doors, then set himself to the task of swiftly divesting himself of his own clothes. *All* of them.

Amber had once wondered what he would look like naked. Soon, she knew. He was impressive, but slightly scary. A big, strong male animal who could take her more fragile female form and fashion it to his body at will. In that dim light and that confined space, he looked extra-dark and extra-large.

While some inner primitive instinct thrilled at his powerful virility, at the same time there remained a core of fear which was also strangely exciting. Was that passion on his face, or anger? Did she care, as long as he gave her what she now craved? He'd brought her to this point and there was no turning back.

'No!' he said harshly, reaching to stop her when she went to unzip her dress. 'I like you like that. It's far sexier.'

Sexier than being naked?

Yes, it was. She had to agree when she thought about it. Very sexy to have her womanhood bare beneath her skirt. To know he could lift it at any time and she was accessible to him. She wanted to lift it for him now, wanted to lie down and spread her legs and...

Her cheeks burnt with her thoughts, and her heart pounded harder than ever. She reached out to run her hands down over his bare chest, feeling the steely muscles beneath his hair-roughened skin. She slid her hands back upwards, scraping her nails across his flat male breasts with their small, taut nipples.

'No,' he growled. Grabbing her waist, he abruptly lifted her, then turned her round to face the back window, settling her on the seat in a kneeling position. He spread her arms along the top of the seat and curved her fingers over the edge in a tight grip. The position pressed her naked breasts against the soft, cool leather, making her fiercely aware of their heat and their acutely aroused state.

Did she comply out of shock, or mindless desire? A little of both. She was certainly stunned when he lifted her skirt from behind and tucked it into her waist. She simply could not move, could not say a word. She remained still and speechless, her muscles stiffly held, her eyes wide as she stared, dry mouthed, through the back window.

'Beautiful,' he murmured as he began caressing her bare buttocks and the backs of her thighs. Amber moaned and lowered her mouth to the seat. Perversely, her bending arched her back and raised her bottom further for him to touch.

And touch it he did. Teasingly. Tantalisingly. Intimately.

Those clever, devilish hands finally moved to push her legs apart and she began to quake. She had never experienced anything so intensely erotic as the last five minutes. Her breathing had grown ragged with excitement, and as she panted her hardened nipples rubbed arousingly against the leather seat. She had never felt so turned on, or so wickedly sexy in all her life. Her body burned. Her thighs trembled. Her bottom writhed, pouted, invited.

'Ben, please,' she pleaded.

She gasped when he moulded his nude body around hers, his large arms covering hers, his mouth hot against her ear.

'Tell me what you want,' he rasped. 'Say it.'

'Just you,' she groaned.

'But you don't really want *me*, Amber,' he flung at her savagely. 'You only want *this* part.'

She cried out at the brutal abruptness of his penetration, then groaned when he began to pump powerfully into her. She bit her tongue and tried to think, but all coherent thought had long been lost. Her eyes squeezed shut and she gripped the seat. But soon her own body was rocking backwards and forwards in counterpoint with his. It was a savage rhythm, a wildly erotic dance which was as compelling as it was uncontrollable.

The top of her head almost came off when her body burst into a climax fiercer than any she'd ever known. Ben's followed almost immediately, and it was while they were violently in spasm together that he turned her face around and covered his mouth with hers.

It might have been one final domineering act, but it wasn't that kind of kiss. He moaned into her mouth, then shuddered as their tongues met. Amber's whole being jolted with a flash of emotional lightning. She knew then that this mating had not been a matter of just sex, but a deeply bonding experience for both of them. All those ghosts from the past had finally been laid to rest, and now...now they could go forward.

Her hand reached up to stroke his cheek. Gently. Lovingly. The gesture seemed to bother him, for his mouth stilled, then lifted. His eyes were almost disbelieving as they stared down into her love-glazed eyes.

'My darling,' was all she said. But it seemed to be enough. For when he kissed her again his lips were full of love and tenderness.

Their bodies gradually grew calm and they slumped sidewards on the seat, still fused. Finally, Amber had to turn her face back to the front, or risk breaking her neck.

'Hold me?' she asked him.

He did, arms wrapped tightly around her.

'Talk to me.'

'About what?'

'Anything. Everything. Tell me you love me.'

She felt him freeze. But she went boldly on, spurred by the courage of her convictions. He loved her. She knew he did.

'Because I love you, Ben. I think I've always loved you. I just didn't know it at the time.'

'Amber, stop joking with me.'

'I'm not joking. I'm deadly serious.'

His silence was electric.

'Don't you love me, Ben?' she asked at last, feeling sick to her stomach that she might have just made the biggest mistake in her life—even bigger than marrying Chad.

His sigh was long and weary-sounding. 'You know I do.'

Her own sigh carried enormous relief. 'That's all right, then. So when are we going to get married?'

'When I ask you,' he bit out.

'Oh. Oh, all right. It's just a male ego thing, is it? So when are you going to ask me? Later tonight? Tomorrow morning? Or are you going to tease me and make me wait a whole week or two?'

'You are the most exasperating female!'

'And the happiest. Oh, Ben, I've never felt anything like that. Never, ever.'

'Not even with your ex-husband?'

'Especially not with him.'

'You didn't love him, Amber?'

'No.'

'Then why did you marry him?'

'For all the wrong reasons.'

'Are we talking about money here?'

'Not really. Though I dare say it played a part. As did charm and flattery and buckets of attention. Chad pursued me across half the world. He was fifteen years older than me, and just swept me off my feet. You have to remember, I was only eighteen when I first met him. He told me he would give me the world if I married him.

'I was utterly bowled over by the thought that this handsome, rich, experienced man loved me so much and so obsessively. It was a very heady feeling, having someone so crazy about you after feeling all your life that no one ever really loved you or cared about you. When he said he'd just die if I didn't marry him, I believed him. I didn't realise Chad's idea of love and marriage didn't tally with my own.'

'In what way?' Ben asked.

'For one thing, he didn't want children. He'd actually had a vasectomy. But I didn't know that till the ring was on my finger. As his wife, all I was required to do was look beautiful all the time, flatter his considerable ego and give him sex whenever he wanted it. Perhaps if I'd slept with him before the wedding I would have realised Chad could never make me happy.'

'Why *didn't* you sleep with him before the wedding?'

'I just didn't want to—which should have rung warning bells. Yet, perversely, I think my reluctance to sleep with him made him all the more keen.'

'Did he think you were still a virgin?'

'No. I'd told him there'd been someone else, someone who'd hurt me. And that I was wary of being hurt again.'

Ben groaned. 'Don't remind me, Amber. That night has haunted me all my life. You've no idea how sorry I am about the way I treated you. Even if you *hadn't* been a virgin, I had no right to say the things I did. They were hypocritical and cruel.'

'I was pretty hypocritical and cruel myself later that night. But let's not go over that old ground any more, Ben. I want to go forward. We all make mistakes when we're young and stupid. Just look at my marriage to Chad!'

'Wasn't sex ever any good with him?'

Amber sighed. 'Not really. Oh, he did try hard to

satisfy me. I'll give him that. Once, in a pink fit, I had a climax of sorts, but it wasn't very memorable and never during actual sex. He blamed me, of course. And he was right. I didn't love him. That was the problem right from the start.'

'Why didn't you leave him?'

'At first I didn't because I felt so guilty. He loved me so much. And he was so good to me. I didn't want to hurt him. Unfortunately, he thought the way to my heart was to lavish presents on me. Designer clothes. Jewellery. Fancy holidays. Maybe there are some women who find that kind of thing an aphrodisiac but I didn't. It just made me feel awful, and even more guilty. Gradually he stopped trying to please me in any way in bed, and sex was just for his pleasure, never for mine. He became very demanding, and God help me if I didn't give him whatever he wanted.'

'You mean he would hit you if you refused him?'

'Not actually. But he was very threatening. He began calling me names. He often locked me in my room while he went out all night. Then, when he came home the next morning, he would tell me he'd been with a real woman who knew how to treat her man. That kind of thing.'

'My God, the man was a monster!'

'He'd been very spoiled all his life. His money had always bought him whatever he wanted. He couldn't handle the fact that it couldn't buy my total love and enslavement to his wishes. He loved me and hated me at the same time. He could be very nice one day, then horrible the next. He used to like me to dress very sexily when he took me out, but when other men took notice of me he'd accuse me of all sorts of things.'

'I can't understand why you stayed with him and put up with such treatment. That's not like you, Amber.'

'I know. I don't understand it either, looking back. But I just couldn't leave him. I found I didn't have the confidence. By the time things got really bad, he'd made me feel a total failure. My self-esteem was shot to pieces. I was a nervous wreck and drinking quite heavily. He encouraged me to drink right from the start, saying it would relax me. It didn't, but it did make me not care so much.

'It was also the only way I could face his constant sexual demands. I used to feel like a zombie most of the time. I had no will-power. No energy. I have no idea why he liked having sex with me so much. It must have been like sleeping with the dead.'

'My God, Amber, that's terrible. So how did you finally get away from him?'

'Would you believe me if I said it was Chad actually hitting me one night which did the trick? You'd think just the opposite would have happened—that I would have been more cowed than ever. But it didn't work out that way. We'd just come home from a long evening at a Las Vegas casino. Chad had lost a veritable fortune and he was in a vile temper. I must have said something to annoy him and he hit me. I should have been shocked, but I wasn't. The actual physical violence seemed to give me a strange strength. I told him then and there that I was leaving him.'

'And he just let you go?'

'God, no. He put his hands around my throat and almost strangled me. I think when I passed out he finally realised what he was doing and stopped. When I came round he'd gone out for the night. I packed my bags and left. My only communication with him since then has been through lawyers.'

'I'd like to kill the bastard.'

'You don't have to. From what I've heard he's slowly killing himself with booze and drugs. His money's almost run out too.'

'Good.'

'But I don't want to talk about him any more. I want to talk about you.'

'What about me?'

'You're a wonderful lover.'

'Flattery will get you everywhere,' he said, his arms tightening around her. He shifted his whole body a little, the movement reminding Amber that Ben was still inside her. Not only inside her, but on the rise again. She shifted her bottom a little to make sure.

'Oh, yes,' she groaned when the sensation of fullness was repeated.

'Oh, yes, what?' he whispered.

'Oh, yes, I want you to do it again.'

'Do what again?'

'You know what. Don't tease me.'

'Would I do that to you?' he said, and started a slow and deliciously pleasurable rhythm.

'Yes.'

'But you're so lovely to tease. You get so frantic, and so…abandoned.'

She groaned. 'Don't remind me.'

'No need to be embarrassed. I love you like that.'

'But I get so hot. And I can't seem to think straight.'

'I wasn't too cool-headed myself. You don't honestly think I make a habit of practising unsafe sex, do you?'

'I certainly hope not,' she reproved, then gasped as he contacted a very sensitive spot. God, but he was good at this. 'What…what are we going to do if I get pregnant?'

'Run.'

'Run! Whatever for?'

'To keep in front of that father of yours with his big shotgun.'

'My father would be thrilled if I had a baby. And he would be simply mad about any man who married me and made me happy.'

'Oh, well, in that case,' he murmured, 'I think some more happiness is called for.' His already roving right hand slid from where it was cupping her right breast, down over her stomach and into the V of damp curls between her legs, seeking out the highly sensitive nub of flesh which hid there.

Amber bit her bottom lip when he started doing to

it what he'd earlier done to her nipples, running erotic circles around the base but without directly touching any of the exquisitely responsive nerve-endings.

'Oh, God,' she choked out, her body trembling with her suddenly acute state of sexual tension.

'You don't like that?'

'Yes. No. It's lovely, but it…it drives me crazy.'

'That's what it's supposed to do.'

'Bastard.'

'Yes, I know. I am. Literally.'

'*Are* you?' Amber asked, momentarily distracted from that tantalising finger. 'I didn't know that.'

'How do you think I ended up with the same sur-name as Gran? Yes, I'm the sorry product of a one-night stand. My mother was an alcoholic who was anyone's when she drank. But that's another story, and a rather boring one. Now, do shut up the chit-chat, sweetness. I have other plans for now.'

He began surging into her quite seriously. At the same time his finger suddenly centred on the apex of her sensitivity. Amber's buttocks contracted violently. So did every internal muscle she owned.

'Ben,' she said breathlessly. 'I…I'll come if you keep doing that.'

'That's all right,' he groaned, and kept on doing it. 'I'm just about to join you.'

CHAPTER ELEVEN

BEN grinned as he watched Amber sneak up the front steps of the Hollingsworth mansion, a sodden shoe—rescued from the tide—in each hand, her hair a mess, her dress rumpled. She looked like a naughty teenager coming home well after hours.

And yet it wasn't much past midnight. Even so, she'd made him promise to roll his car down the hill before turning on the engine so that her father wouldn't hear.

So much for her saying her father wouldn't come after him with a shotgun if he got his precious darling pregnant out of wedlock. Ben knew Edward Hollingsworth would not be at all pleased. It was as well he had every intention of marrying the girl. He also had every intention of making her pregnant. Amber wasn't going to get away from him a second time!

She turned and blew him a kiss before tiptoeing round the side of the house towards the back.

Ben smiled all the way down the hill. He had never felt so happy. Amber loved him. She wanted to marry him. She wanted to have his children. With a bit of luck, a little Sinclair might already be on the way. Ben had not used protection once during the last couple of hours.

A jab of guilt struck for a second over the thoughts which had gone through his head during that first torrid mating. But he dismissed it quickly. Amber didn't know that he'd been in an agony of bitter resentment at the time, thinking she didn't love him, that all she wanted from him was sex.

So that was what he'd given her for a while. Just sex. No eye contact. No warmth or real intimacy. It hadn't been till she'd touched him on the cheek the way she had—with such tenderness and emotion—that he recognised his mistake, and appreciated the depth of her feelings for him.

Luckily, it wasn't too late. But he might easily have lost her again, he conceded ruefully. That ingrained cynicism and distrust of his had almost tarnished what had ultimately been the most wonderful moment of his life.

He vowed never to distrust Amber's motives again. Or her love for him. For it had undoubtedly been her love which had allowed her to give herself so willingly to him. And so uninhibitedly. She had been incredible in her stunning surrender to his wishes. Not to mention in her implicit faith in him. She'd placed herself totally in his hands tonight and trusted him not to hurt her.

He was so relieved that he hadn't. Either emotionally or physically. Especially after what she'd told him about that bastard she'd been married to.

But it had been a close call.

He shook his head at himself as he drove home

along the winding valley road. He was still shaking his head when he rounded the final corner and saw the smoke.

It was coming from the farm.

Ben's foot went down hard to the floor as a thousand sickening needles stabbed him. The car leapt forward, the tyres screeching on the tar.

It wasn't the house burning, he realised with some relief as he sped nearer. The smoke was coming from behind it. It had to be the old barn.

Ben's relief would have been greater if it hadn't been for the police car parked outside the rickety front fence. The presence of the police suggested the fire hadn't been some silly accident. As he drew closer Ben could see the barn had been levelled to a smouldering heap.

Gran's old blue utility, which was usually housed in the barn, was safely parked out at the front, so it looked as if the fire had happened while Gran had been at her club.

Ben tried to keep too many terrible thoughts from crowding in, but as he swung his car to face the front fence the headlights beamed across the house, illuminating the red-painted words which defaced the walls.

'NEXT TIME WE'LL BURN THE HOUSE!' decorated the left side of the front door.

'GET THE HELL OUT, YOU SELFISH OLD WITCH!' was spelt out on the right.

Ben felt sick to his stomach. He'd always known

the world had its fair share of low-life, but this was something else. To bully and terrify a poor, defence-less old lady! He couldn't imagine what Gran had thought and felt when she'd come home from the club.

His anger was mixed with guilt that he hadn't been here. Instead he'd been…

The most hideous thought struck, making him physically recoil. For a few agonising seconds Ben suffered as he had never suffered before. But then, gradually, his new faith in Amber kicked in and he knew she would not be involved in something so vile. Not his Amber. Not the woman he loved, and who loved him.

But that new faith did not extend to her father! Ben couldn't stop himself from considering the possibility that his dinner invitation to the Hollingsworths' tonight had had an ulterior motive from the word go, or that Edward Hollingsworth had taken advantage of his knowledge that their guest would not be going home for a good while because he was going for a drive with his daughter.

Ben recalled having told Amber's father over din-ner that his gran spent every Saturday night down at the club playing bingo and other games. He also re-called how his host had cried exhaustion straight after dinner and bolted for his room. Had he immediately called some henchman of his and given him the green light to go down to the farm and do his worst?

Ben had to admit he'd be surprised at Edward

Hollingsworth's seemingly easy capitulation over the farm. That was not like him. Amber's father had always been known as a hard-headed businessman who cut whatever corners needed to be cut, and wouldn't shrink from the odd spot of bribery and corruption. Maybe some of that was exaggeration, or sour grapes, but Ben had always found that bad reputations had usually been earned.

He'd had one himself as a youngster, and he'd certainly deserved every rotten thing people had said about him. He also knew that he owed where he was today to his gran's faith that underneath the sulky, antisocial adolescent had lain a decent boy with a good brain and a good heart.

Dear Gran. She had never faltered in her love and faith in him. Never!

Hell, what was he doing sitting here in his car when he should be inside, giving her comfort, telling her he would not leave her to face this alone?

Ben was out of his car like a shot. He hurdled the front gate and was racing up the front steps when a large policeman pushed through the wire door.

Sergeant Peterson was in his late fifties, and had been the head honcho at the Sunrise Point police station for as long as Ben had been around town. He was a tough customer—he'd frightened the hell out of Ben the first day he'd arrived—but he was straight as a die. The world could do with a lot of policemen like Sergeant Peterson.

'Glad to see you, Ben,' he said straight away.

'Nasty business, this. I had your gran taken to the hospital. Now don't panic, lad. She'll be okay. Just a bit of a turn. Shock, plus a touch of angina. It was the firemen finding the dog that did it.'

'The dog?' Ben repeated, then groaned as the penny dropped. 'Oh, dear God, they didn't harm poor old Rocky, did they? He wouldn't hurt a flea!'

'Yes, I know—despite that interesting article in the local paper,' the policeman said drily. 'To be honest, I don't think they meant to hurt the dog. It seemed your gran locked the animal in the barn before going off to the club. She told me he'd started following her and she was worried he might get run over, it being Saturday night and all. I doubt the would-be arsonists even knew the dog was in there when they threw the Molotov cocktail into the barn.'

'He's dead,' Ben said flatly.

'Afraid so.'

Ben sank down onto the front steps and put his head into his hands. God knew why he would want to cry over a stupid old dog. Rocky wasn't even *his* dog. But cry he did, his shoulders shaking as the tears started streaming down his face.

The policeman put a comforting hand on his shoulder but said nothing, just waited till Ben could pull himself together. Which he did, after a few minutes.

'Sorry about that,' Ben muttered, and took another deep breath as he stood up. 'So! Do you have any idea who the guilty party or parties might be?'

'I have an interesting tyre-track to go on. Plus a

couple of empty spray cans. I reckon it won't take me too long to find out, especially once the townsfolk get to hear about this. I don't think too many were on your gran's side last week—after all, a new cinema and shopping complex could be just what the doctor ordered for this town—but no one likes this kind of tactic. And neither do I!'

'Well, I can give you a pretty good idea where to look first,' Ben ground out caustically. 'Let me give you his address!'

'I knew you'd think that. But you're wrong. Ed Hollingsworth wouldn't do anything like this. Oh, I know he used to be a wheeler-dealer, with little respect for fair play, but that was way in the past. The man's changed.'

'Yeah, right,' Ben said sarcastically.

'Are you saying people can't change?' the policeman challenged. 'I would have thought you of all people would be prepared to give others the benefit of the doubt. After all, the boy who came to live in this town back in the eighties was well on his way to being a criminal. If it wasn't for Pearl you'd have a record for car-stealing. But she begged that judge to give you a second chance and he did. You can thank your lucky stars he did too, otherwise you wouldn't have become a lawyer. You'd have been either a crook or a bum!'

Ben said nothing, and Sergeant Peterson sighed. 'Look, I'll go speak to Ed first thing in the morning. But I'd bet my superannuation he's innocent of this.'

Ben wished that were the case, but he doubted it.

Either Sergeant Peterson was naive, or Ben had been wrong in his character assessment. He hoped against hope he wasn't going to be very disappointed in this man whom he'd always admired and respected.

'Edward Hollingsworth is hardly going to confess, even if he *is* guilty,' Ben said, trying to keep the cynicism out of his voice. 'Okay, I'll try to give him the benefit of the doubt. So who else do you think might have done this?'

'My guess would be one of the tradesmen or building contractors who might have stood to make quite a bit of money out of such a large property development. You've no idea, Ben, just how bad things have been around here.'

'I think I have,' he returned drily as he glared at the vandalised house.

The policeman nodded wearily. 'Yeah. I know what you mean. It's a sad state of affairs.'

'It's a bloody disgrace!' Ben growled. 'And worthy of headlines in more papers than some pathetic local *Gazette*!'

'God, Ben, please don't go to the city papers,' the policeman pleaded. 'The last thing this town needs is bad press. Without tourism we'd be totally dead in the water.'

'What do I care about this damned town now? My gran and her safety are all I care about!'

'That's bulldust and you know it, Ben. You're not nearly as tough as you make out. Besides, you wouldn't want to do anything to spoil your chances with Amber Hollingsworth, would you?'

Ben just stared at him.

The policeman shrugged his big, beefy shoulders. 'You can't keep too many secrets in this town. Word is you went to dinner at her place tonight. Was that a rumour or a fact?'

'A fact.'

His thick eyebrows arched as he glanced at his watch. 'Pretty long dinner.'

'I went for a drive afterwards.'

'Pretty long drive.'

'I wasn't alone.'

'Don't tell me. Ed went with you. Or was it Beverly?'

'Very funny.'

'Yeah, well, I'm a laugh a minute. Now, I'd better get on with solving this case and I suggest you get down to the hospital and see your gran. But just a friendly word of warning before you go.'

'What?'

'Don't go opening your mouth about this to all and sundry and putting your foot right in it. For one thing, that little lady ain't going to like you smearing her daddy's name all round town. She thinks the sun shines out of him.'

Ben grimaced at this unexpected complication to his new relationship with Amber. The sergeant was right. She wouldn't take well to his accusing her father of such a crime. She would see that as evidence of Ben still having a nasty, suspicious mind. Which admittedly he did, when the object of his suspicions was worthy of it!

Sergeant Peterson clamped a firm hand over his shoulder. 'Let the law do its job, lad.'

Ben scowled. 'Where I come from, the law doesn't always *do* its damned job.'

'Then perhaps you're living in the wrong town.'

'Somehow this isn't the moment to tell me that,' Ben muttered, and stalked off.

His Gran was in a room by herself. She looked very small in the high hospital bed. And very pale.

Her eyes were closed when Ben tiptoed in and pulled up a chair. But no sooner had he sat down than she opened her eyes and turned her face towards him.

'Hi, there, Gran,' he said gently. 'How are you feeling?'

'Like I should be feeling,' she said faintly. 'Rocky's dead, you know.'

'Yeah,' he said, swallowing. 'I know.'

'It's all my fault. All my fault...'

Ben could hardly bear it when her eyes suddenly flooded and two big tears rolled down her cheeks. He took her nearest hand and squeezed it. 'No, Gran. That's not true. Nothing that happened tonight was your fault.'

'Oh, yes, it was,' she said, nodding slowly. 'I'm just getting what I deserved. ''Selfish old witch'', they painted on my wall. And they're right. I am. And now my poor old Rocky is dead. Better it was me who was dead. I'm the one who deserved it.'

'Gran, don't,' Ben choked out. 'It wasn't your fault. Truly.'

She just looked at him, no longer crying. But her face was so unhappy. 'You don't understand. And I simply can't tell you. I don't want you to look at me like you hate me.'

'Gran, don't be silly; I could never hate you. I love you.'

Her eyes welled up anew, and more tears rolled down her wrinkled cheeks. But her voice was oddly calm as she spoke.

'I want you to ring the Hollingsworths in the morning and tell them I want to sell.'

Ben's first reaction was an instinctive negative. Didn't she understand that was what the bastard wanted? To break her spirit and force her to sell?

He was about to tell her be damned with that. They would stand and fight together. But then he saw the reality of her age and her health, and remained broodingly silent.

'I...I don't want to ever go back there...to the farm. I'll find myself a place in one of them retirement villages. They tell me there's some good ones up at Coffs Harbour.'

'Coffs Harbour! Why would you want to move up there? You like it here in Sunrise. This is your home!'

'Oh, I couldn't stay here. Not now.'

'Then you can come to Sydney and live with me. I could easily sell my unit and buy a nice little—'

'No,' she broke in firmly. 'Thank you, Ben, but no. I don't want you to do that. Now I would like to go to sleep, dear. I feel very tired.'

Ben sighed. He felt pretty tired himself, all of a sudden. It had been a long night.

'All right, Gran,' he said, patting her hand. 'I'll see you in the morning.'

He hated leaving her but common sense prevailed. The doctor had said she was basically fine. She just needed some peace and quiet after the shocks of the evening.

Ben was somewhat perturbed, however, by her obvious depression and guilt over Rocky's death. Clearly she blamed herself for some reason. Maybe she was thinking of that article in the paper, and that little white lie about Rocky being a vicious dog.

But, damn it all, the dog's death still wasn't *her* fault. *She* hadn't burnt the damn barn down! With a bit of luck, she would see that in time.

Ben also hoped he could talk her out of this silly idea about running away to Coffs Harbour to live. She'd be miserable away from all her old friends, *and* without a private place of her own.

Ben drove back to the farm, feeling pretty depressed himself. There he'd been earlier, on top of the world, confident of his future happiness. Now he wasn't so sure things would work out quite so easily for himself and Amber. He toyed with the idea of calling her when he got home. But it was two in the morning and her battleaxe of a stepmother would probably answer the telephone.

It was a pity Amber lived at home, he decided. If she'd had a place of her own he could have gone there now. He really wanted to be with her, he wanted to put his arms around her and lose himself in her warmth and her love.

But being with her would have to wait till tomorrow.

Meanwhile, he had no option but to see if he could get a few hours' sleep.

It would not be easy, Ben conceded as he swung his car in to face the house and saw the ugly graffiti a second time. Hard not to well up with resentment over who could do such a disgusting thing. Hard not to imagine Edward Hollingsworth had had a hand in it.

He stood to gain the most, after all. The most money. The most acclaim around town.

Ben wouldn't put it past the bastard to run for Mayor again after the complex was up and running. He'd always coveted that position. He'd run for it before enough damned times. Unsuccessfully. Till now.

Ben gritted his teeth at the thought that someone would prosper over a dog's death and an old lady's despair.

He'd be damned if he would turn a blind eye! Not even for Amber.

His bitter resolve was deepened when he walked round the back to the burned-out barn and saw what had once been Rocky. No way did he believe that whoever had burnt that barn hadn't known the dog was there. Rocky would have barked.

There were no more tears, however, as he dug a grave and buried the dog. Only a hardened heart and a determination not to let the perpetrator of this crime totally get away with it.

Okay, he would not go to the papers. But he aimed to confront Amber's father and see for himself what the man had to say in his defence.

Ben knew he would be risking Amber's love in doing that. She might even hate him for it. But he knew he would hate himself more if he just put his head in the sand and pretended he did not believe what he believed. If the man *was* innocent, let him prove it. Let him look Ben in the eye and swear to him he'd had nothing to do with this shameful act.

Ben was used to dealing with liars. He had a knack nowadays for recognising their body language. He believed he would know the truth when he saw it. And he would see it tomorrow—whatever it was, and wherever it led.

CHAPTER TWELVE

AMBER woke with the dawn. For a while she just lay there in bed, thinking about the night before and the incredible turn of events.

Ben loved her. *Really* loved her. And she really loved him in return. It wasn't just sex—though heaven knew that part of it was wonderful. What they now shared was something far deeper than a physical attraction, even though Amber still believed a very special connection had begun all those years ago when they'd first met.

They had been kindred spirits from the start, drawn to each other despite the barriers society threw up between them. Two lonely souls reaching out to each other for love.

The only problem was they hadn't known how to love back then. They'd only known how to want, and to take, and to hurt.

Amber understood now why Ben had hurt her as he had that night. She understood and forgave him, just as she hoped he understood and forgave her.

He certainly seemed to have. He had been so sympathetic and understanding over her relationship with Chad. It had been a great burden off her shoulders to talk about her marriage honestly for once. She had never told anyone the truth because underneath she'd felt it was all somehow her fault, that she'd been a failure as a woman.

Ben had made her see that the blame rested squarely on Chad's shoulders. And what had really thrilled her was that Ben hadn't even *looked* like jumping to any wrong conclusions. There had been no hasty accusations, no harsh judgements, just kindness and sympathy. He'd changed far more than she'd realised. That angry young man who'd always thought the worst of people was no more.

Amber smiled to herself as she thought of their future together. They were going to be so happy. And their children were going to be happy. Her hands moved under the sheet to smooth over her stomach. She'd come to bed naked because she'd wanted to keep alive the memory of Ben's lovemaking, wanted to keep on feeling sexy and slightly wicked.

She wondered if there was anything happening under her flat tummy, if a baby was already growing. She hoped so with all her heart.

Her hands slid up to her breasts and their still tender nipples. She could not wait for Ben to make love to her again. He'd promised to ring her today. She hoped he was as impatient as she was. She didn't want to have to wait till lunchtime for his call!

It was at that moment Amber recalled her intention to move out of home today and into the cottage. What good timing, she thought. Ben could help her, and then, after she was unpacked, and she'd made up the big bed in the main bedroom with clean sheets, they could test out the mattress together!

Flinging back the sheet, she propelled her naked form out of the bed and into the bathroom. There was no time to waste. Not if she wanted the whole afternoon for herself and Ben!

By eight-thirty Amber was dressed in denim shorts and vest, her long hair was sensibly plaited, every suitcase she owned was stuffed with clothes, and a pile of assorted linen was stacked in readiness for the move. Beverly wouldn't miss some sheets and towels. Over the years she had bought more than she and her father could use in ten lifetimes!

As she glanced around her room Amber gave a sigh of satisfaction at how much she'd achieved in a couple of hours. It wasn't even nine o'clock. But by golly she was hungry. She'd worked up a real appetite.

Amber was munching into her second lot of Vegemite toast just after nine when the front doorbell rang. Since everyone else seemed to be sleeping in extra late that Sunday morning, she went to answer it, her coffee mug in hand. Who knew? Maybe it was Ben come to see her, though it was a little early for a personal visit.

The sight of Sergeant Peterson standing on the doorstep was a surprise.

'Goodness, Sarge!' she exclaimed brightly. 'I hope you haven't come to arrest me.'

His smile was strained, and instantly worrying.

Amber frowned. 'There's nothing wrong, is there?'

He looked pained at having to answer her. 'There was some trouble down at the Sinclair farm last night.'

Amber's stomach lurched. 'Nothing's happened to Ben, has it?'

'No, he's fine. But Pearl's in hospital, being treated for shock.'

'My God, what happened?'

'She got home from the club last night to find the old barn burning and some pretty nasty words sprayed across the front of the house.'

'Oh, dear Lord,' Amber groaned. 'Ben said his gran had received several harassing telephone calls. It must be the same person.'

'He seemed to think so,' Sergeant Peterson said on an oddly dry note. 'Unfortunately, when the barn was burned it wasn't empty. Pearl had put her dog in there to stop him from following her to town last night. He died in the fire.'

Amber moaned. 'Oh, God! Poor Pearl! She must be devastated.'

'She didn't take it well. That's why she's in the hospital.'

Amber felt stricken. 'She *is* going to be all right, isn't she?'

'I certainly hope so. I don't know what Ben might do if anything happens to that old lady as well. He thinks the world of her. I had trouble as it was stopping him from going to the newspapers with this. And I'm not talking about the local *Gazette*!'

'He must be terribly upset.'

'That's putting it mildly. When he found out about the dog, he just sat there and cried. Never thought I'd see Ben Sinclair cry; I'll tell you that.'

Amber was close to crying herself, just thinking about it. 'I must go to him straight away.'

'Er...I'm not sure that's a wise move just at the moment, Amber. Give him a chance to cool down, and me a chance to find out who the *real* culprit is.'

Amber frowned. 'What do you mean, "the *real* culprit"? It's perfectly obvious that—'

She broke off suddenly, the reason behind the policeman's presence, plus the horror of what he was implying, finally sinking in. 'Oh, dear God, Ben thinks we did it. The Hollingsworths, that is. That's why you're here!'

'Not you, Amber. But it crossed his mind that your father might be involved. Personally, I don't believe Ed had anything to do with it, but I do have to speak to him in the light of that article in the paper last week. You do see that, Amber?'

'I suppose so,' she said tautly. 'But you and I both know he would never do a thing like that!'

'Who wouldn't do a thing like what?' Beverly asked as she walked downstairs.

The sergeant explained in part, and soon an indignant Beverly was reluctantly taking him down to see the master of the house. Amber used the opportunity to dash back into the kitchen, dump the remains of her toast and grab her car keys. She was racing towards the door into the garages when Beverly grabbed her arm, spinning her to a stop.

'And where do you think *you're* off to?'

'I'm going to see Ben.'

'Oh, I see. You've chosen sides already, have you? Lover-boy in preference to your father and your family.'

'It's not like that, Beverly. Ben and I are in love and—'

'In *love*?' came the sneering remark. 'Don't make me laugh. The only person you love, madam, is yourself. Still, I have to give credit where credit is due. It certainly didn't take dear Ben very long to get into your pants, did it? He must have a lot more going for him than poor old Chad. I guess there are some things money just can't buy.'

Amber felt a wild fury rise in her, much as she had that day Chad had struck her.

'Tell me, Beverly, were you born a right bitch, or did you learn the art along the way?'

'I just say it as I see it,' she sniffed.

'Then let me tell you a few home truths in return. I used to like you. I was genuinely happy when Dad found someone to love after being so lonely all those years. But I see now you're just another of those greedy, grabbing, selfish widows who marry for money and comfort then turn sour when life presents them with a few unexpected problems.

'You weren't bargaining on a sick husband, were you? Only a rich one! And you certainly weren't bargaining on his grown-up daughter coming home to live and interrupting your cushy, lazy, self-indulgent lifestyle. Suddenly that so-called love you supposedly felt for my father wore very thin indeed.'

'That's not true!' Beverly spat at her, her face flushing an angry red. 'I *do* love your father. And he *used* to love me. And talk to me. And rely solely on me. But then *you* came home—his poor, darling, hard-done-by daughter! Suddenly I was shoved aside and it was all Amber, Amber, Amber! After his stroke I began to hope that at last he might need me and turn to me to look after him. But, no! He hired Bill to do that! I hardly see Edward any more. He never confides in me. *No one* around here confides in me. No one gives me any love or respect. Is it any wonder I do the things I do?' she wailed. 'Is it any wonder I've turned into a right bitch?'

Amber just stared at her, hearing the real pain in the woman's voice. Amazingly, she began to understand why her stepmother had been eaten up with jealousy and resentment. Her father had never been large on sensitivity. And he *had* made rather a fuss of Amber when she'd returned.

'Beverly, I'm so sorry,' Amber apologised. 'I don't know what to say. I didn't realise.'

Amber was shocked when tears filled Beverly's eyes.

'Dad does love you,' she added. 'Maybe things will get better when I move out today.'

'You're moving out?'

'Yes. Into a cottage on the other side of town.'

'Edward will be upset,' Beverly muttered. 'He'll probably blame me.'

'No, he won't. I told him last night and he understood.'

'Oh, I see,' she said bitterly. 'You told him, but you didn't tell me. That's so typical.'

'Beverly, be fair. You've hardly been pleasant to me lately.'

Beverly stiffened. 'That doesn't excuse Edward. Why didn't *he* tell me? Why is it that my feelings never matter? He makes me feel such a nothing lately!'

'He's hardly had the opportunity,' Amber argued. 'I only told him very late last night, just before going out with Ben. Which reminds me. I really must go now, Beverly. Whether you believe me or not, this is nothing to do with choosing sides. I love Ben and I aim to marry him. Under the circumstances, I need to get down to the farm straight away and convince him we had nothing to do with what happened there last night, make him see that the Hollingsworths are not murderers!'

'Murderers!' Beverly gasped, all the angry red fading from her face. 'Whatever are you talking about?'

'Didn't Sergeant Peterson tell you what happened?'

'I didn't stay to listen to everything. I gather some threats have been painted on Pearl's house.'

'I see. Well, that wasn't all. Her barn was burnt down and Pearl's dog was in there at the time.'

Beverly looked aghast. 'You...you don't mean the dog was...killed...do you?'

'Yes.'

Now she looked as if she was going to be sick. 'Oh, dear God...'

Amber felt quite touched by her stepmother's obvious shock. It seemed her stepmother had a soft heart underneath that tough bitch image she'd been wearing lately.

'Yes, it's awful, isn't it?' Amber said sympathetically. 'It was finding the dog which put poor Pearl in hospital. Whoever did this has to thank his lucky stars she didn't die of a heart attack as well. Then we'd be looking at manslaughter at least. Look—must go, Beverly, before I miss Ben altogether.'

Amber left a surprisingly pale-faced Beverly behind and hurried out to her car. She knew she had to get to Ben before he worked himself into a real state, and started believing all sorts of other stupid things, even worse than he already did.

The old Ben was sure to be lurking somewhere in his head, and that old Ben might begin to believe she'd lured him out to the beach and let him make love to her for hours to leave the way clear for her father's henchmen to burn his grandmother's barn, kill her dog and deface her home.

Amber could almost cope with Ben's thinking badly of her father.

But not of herself.

Despair played at the edges of her heart as she sped

along the valley road. Please God, she prayed. Please don't let him think awful things about me. Please don't take away his trust in my character. Or his faith in my love. I need him to believe in me.

She rounded the last corner, both relieved and agitated to see Ben's car still parked outside the house. She'd been worried he might have left to go down to the hospital. It would be hard to talk to him there.

She swung her small white sedan in beside the larger black saloon, her heart contracting at the sight of the messages scrawled across the house. How ugly they looked in the sunlight! But how much uglier at night. And much more terrifying. Her heart went out to Ben's gran. But at the same time her own fears escalated. This was the moment of truth.

She switched off the engine and climbed out, her step as hesitant as her heart. What if Ben didn't believe she had nothing to do with this? Bad enough he seemed to believe her father was involved.

With a heavy but pounding heart, she launched her legs towards the gate.

Ben wasn't in the house. It was deserted.

Amber made her way slowly through the back door and immediately saw him over near what had once been the barn. He was driving a rough wooden cross into one end of what looked like a grave.

Seeing the stark evidence of Rocky's death hit Amber hard. Before that moment she'd felt sad about the dog's unfortunate demise. But to actually see that mound of dirt was something else.

Her strangled cry had Ben whirling round. For a long, torturously anguished moment, he just looked at her. But then the axe slipped from his hand to fall to the ground and he began walking back towards the house, crossing the space which separated them with quickening strides.

As he came closer Amber was appalled by the torment in his eyes. Her arms reached out by instinct, and then she was running and crying at the same time.

He gathered her in and hugged her, as though he was afraid she might disappear if he didn't hold her tight. Her heart welled up to bursting point with emotion. He still loved her and believed in her. Not only that, he needed her.

She hugged him back just as fiercely, burying her face into his neck till the tears stopped flowing and the enormous lump in her throat slowly dissolved. Only then did she draw back and cup his face.

'Sergeant Peterson came to the house first thing this morning,' she whispered in answer to the question in his eyes. 'Oh, Ben! I'm so sorry about the dog and everything. I can't begin to think what your gran is thinking and feeling. I'd like to go and visit her in the hospital if that's all right with you.'

'I'm not so sure she would want to see you.'

Her hands dropped away from him in shock. 'She...she doesn't think *I* had anything to do with this, does she?'

He sighed. 'I'm not sure what Gran thinks. She hasn't said all that much. She did ask me to tell you and your father that the farm's yours. She doesn't want to come back to live here. Ever! She's talking about going right away, to live in one of those retirement places further up the coast. For some reason she seems to think this is all her fault.'

'But that's crazy!'

'Gran is a lot of things,' he said drily, 'but crazy is not one of them. I'm not sure what's behind her reasoning, but she's very depressed about Rocky. And full of the strangest guilt. Nothing I said last night seemed to make any impression. She was oddly content to take all this on her own poor shoulders. God knows why. Perhaps she thinks she should have sold to you straight away, no matter what she wanted for herself. She said she agreed with what was written on the house—that she *was* a selfish old witch.'

'Oh, Ben, that's dreadful.'

'Yes, it is,' he bit out. 'This whole scenario is damned dreadful. Look, I won't beat around the bush, Amber. I think your father had some hand in this. It's just all too coincidental for my liking. I get an invite to dinner and this happens while I'm away.'

'You're wrong, Ben. But you have a right to your opinion. And I understand it. I really do.'

'You do?' He seemed amazed at her attitude. But she was only telling him the truth. She *did* understand.

'I would probably think the same in your shoes. I'm just glad that you don't think I was in any way involved.'

'I never thought that for a moment.'

She smiled at him. 'Ben, you're a wonderful liar.'

'Yeah, well, okay, so the possibility did cross my mind for a second. But only for a second; I swear it. I only had to think of the wonderfully warm way you kissed me goodnight last night and I knew you couldn't have been a party to something so underhanded. You would have to be really bad, and the woman I love is not even remotely bad.'

She reached up on tiptoes and kissed him on his stubbly cheek. 'I love you all the more for having faith in me. And being totally honest. I want you to always be honest with me, Ben, and I promise you the same in return.'

'That's sounds good to me. I've spent too many of my last years dealing with people whose idea of honesty is what they can get away with.'

'Ben, don't go back to Sydney,' she urged, taking his hand as they walked together back to the house. 'Stay here in Sunrise with me. You can open up a legal practice here. There isn't a solicitor under sixty in town—just a couple of old codgers who'll be retired soon. Your gran wouldn't want to move away either, if she thought you were going to live here.'

'I don't know about that. She didn't want to go to Sydney and live with me when I asked her. As for staying here, Amber... I do like the idea, but I'm not sure I'd want to live so close to your father after this.'

'What if Sergeant Peterson can prove it wasn't Dad?'

'What if he can't?' he countered bitterly.

'If he can't, I'll go to Sydney with you. I'll go wherever you want me to go. I love you, Ben, and I want to be with you.'

He gave her another hug. 'You don't know how much your saying that means to me.'

'I probably won't have to do it once you find out my father is innocent.'

Ben drew back from her embrace, shaking his head. 'They say love is blind.'

'My love is not at all blind,' she argued. 'I've known my father for nearly thirty years, and I *know* he didn't do this—just as I know that underneath your bad-boy, tough-guy image you're really a deeply feeling and sensitive man.'

Ben stared at her for a full thirty seconds. Then he nodded slowly. 'Very well, Amber. I'll accept that you probably know your father better than I do. I also appreciate that, under the law, he's innocent till proven guilty. But I want to see what he has to say for himself. Will you drive me over there? I'm a little shot this morning.'

Amber went weak at the knees at this snap decision. 'You want to go visit Dad now? This very minute?'

'Yes, this very minute,' he said in steely tones. 'Why? What's the problem? Having doubts, all of a sudden?'

Her chin came up. 'In my father? Never!'

'Let's go, then.'

CHAPTER THIRTEEN

AMBER'S father had not been at home. Neither had
his wife. Or Bill, his minder. The house had been
deserted.

Amber and Ben had looked at each other and simultaneously said, 'They've gone to the hospital!'

Now Ben was guiding Amber along the corridor
which led to his gran's room, and he was feeling more
uncertain than at any time in his life before. The ward
sister had just informed them that his grandmother did
have visitors at the moment. A man in a wheelchair
and a lady. Bill, it seemed, must have stayed with the
car. Or outside somewhere.

Had the Hollingsworths come in a friendly fashion?
Ben worried. Were they here out of sympathy and
kindness, or just to selfishly try to avoid another scandal in the papers?

Ben could not associate Beverly Hollingsworth
with kindness or sympathy. As for her husband... Ben
sincerely hoped both Sergeant Peterson and Amber
were right about him. But he'd been cynical too long
to have blind faith in another man.

Suddenly Amber gave his hand a comforting
squeeze, and he glanced over at her. 'It'll be all right,
Ben. I just know it.'

'God, I hope so. And I hope that stepmother of yours hasn't already put her foot in her mouth.'

'She certainly wouldn't win any prizes lately for her tact,' Amber agreed ruefully. 'But I saw a side of her this morning which makes me hope she might be on the improve.'

'Really?'

'Yes, really. She was most upset over what happened at the farm—especially when I told her about poor Rocky.'

Amber's surprising new opinion of her stepmother seemed to be confirmed when they came to the open doorway of his gran's room and Ben saw Beverly standing next to Gran's bed, arranging the most beautiful big bunch of roses in a vase.

'Now you just concentrate on getting yourself well, Pearl,' she was saying. 'That's all she has to do—isn't that right, Edward?'

'Absolutely right, Bev,' Edward echoed. 'And we don't want to hear any more of this nonsense about selling up and moving away from Sunrise. We both know that's not what you really want. Ben told us so last night. Hollingsworths will survive without your land. We'll just have to build the complex somewhere else, that's all.'

'But that's not what I want at all!' Pearl cried. 'I...I can't go back and live in that house. Not now. Not after what happened to poor old Rocky.'

'Why not?' Edward asked.

'Because it was all my fault,' she sobbed, lifting a

handful of crumpled tissues to her mouth. 'I've been a selfishly wicked old woman, and now God is punishing me.'

Ben had heard enough. He dropped Amber's hand and stalked into the room. 'God is *not* punishing you, Gran. And none of this is your fault. The only wickedly selfish person in all this is the one who sent that creep to do what he did last night. Sergeant Peterson says he should be able to trace the culprit from some tyre-tracks, and I feel pretty sure that kind of low-life won't go to jail without dobbing in the person who paid him!'

Ben delivered this veiled threat while glaring at Amber's father. He was astonished when the man looked him back straight in the eye without a qualm. If he was the guilty party, then he was the best damned poker player Ben had ever encountered.

Ben was even more astonished when Beverly Hollingsworth suddenly burst into tears.

Everyone turned to stare at her.

'I didn't mean for anyone to get hurt,' she sobbed.

'My God, Beverly!' Edward exclaimed, ashen-faced. 'Are you saying *you* are responsible for what happened?'

'I…I just wanted to help you get that land after Amber stuffed everything up,' she wailed. 'I thought if Hollingsworths had to abandon the complex this whole town would just keep on going downhill and everyone would blame you and then you would never get to be Mayor. I wanted to make you happy,

Edward. I wanted to be of use to you again. You never seem to need me these days. I believed you when you said all Pearl wanted was more money. I never for a moment thought she would be this upset. Or that her dog would die…'

'Oh, Beverly…Beverly…' Her husband began shaking his head, looking very old and unwell.

Ben actually felt sorry for him. Oddly, he also almost felt sorry for Beverly, who immediately slumped into a chair in the corner and began to weep uncontrollably. She looked very alone and utterly wretched. Ben felt proud of Amber when she walked over and put a comforting arm around her stepmother's shoulders. Beverly's blonde head jerked up and she gave her stepdaughter a shocked look.

'I know you didn't mean for anything really bad to happen,' Amber comforted.

'I didn't,' Beverly choked out. 'I swear. Oh, Pearl, please forgive me. I…I paid this man who used to do my lawns. He's on the dole and was hoping to get a job at the new complex, so he had his own axe to grind. But he was only supposed to spray-paint something on the front fence. When I heard about the fire and your dog I was so shocked. But it was too late then. I will do anything to make it up to you. Anything at all! But please…don't send me to jail!'

Ben's gaze swung to his gran, who was looking at the woman with surprising pity.

'It's all right, Beverly,' Pearl said wearily. 'I won't send you to jail. *Or* the man you hired. I have no intention of pressing charges. And I do understand. Really, I do. We can all do dreadful things when we get older and feel lonely and unwanted and useless. You're not the only guilty party here. I share your blame in Rocky's death. I set this disgraceful affair in motion. I've behaved like a stupid old fool and I can't go on without confessing the truth.'

She turned to look beseechingly at Ben, her face totally crestfallen. 'I only hope you can forgive me, Ben. And you, Edward. And especially you, Amber. I involved you all. And hurt you all. But I ended up hurting myself more. Poor Rocky...' Her eyes swam with new tears.

Ben stepped forward, his heart tightening at her distress. 'Gran, don't. I—'

'No, Ben,' she broke in, blinking furiously as her chin shot up. Her spine and shoulders straightened as she tried to gather herself. 'This confession is mine and mine alone. Let me make it with dignity.' She opened her mouth, then closed it again. She bit her bottom lip and her chin began to wobble. 'Oh, dear. I...I don't think I can tell you after all.'

Amber left her stepmother to come forward to the side of the bed, her lovely blue eyes full of compassion as she took one of Gran's hands in both of hers. Ben could only watch her and marvel at this wonderful woman who loved him.

'Of course you can,' she said warily. 'You can tell us anything. We're all going to be family now.'

'Family?' Pearl echoed faintly.

'Yes. Ben and I are going to be married. And Ben is going to stay here in Sunrise too. He's not going back to Sydney.'

Gran's glistening gaze was wide upon him. 'Is…is that true, Ben?'

'Sure is, Gran.'

'Oh, dear.' Her hands fluttered up to her throat as she struggled to control a new flood of tears. 'I…I never dreamt. Never hoped. It's all my prayers come true.'

'It's all my prayers come true too,' Amber added touchingly. 'I've been in love with Ben from the first day I saw him. I was just too stupid to realise it.'

'And Ben has loved you for just as long,' his gran said. 'And he too was too stupid to realise it.'

'Gran!'

'It's true, Ben. I used to listen to you come home from school and grumble your head off about Amber, but you didn't fool me for a minute. I knew you were stuck on her. Then, when you saved every cent for months to rent that tux for your graduation ball, I knew who it was you wanted to look so grand for. But sadly nothing came of it, and I had to watch you go off to Sydney to study and then to live. And I missed you so much, Ben. I can't tell you how much.'

Ben was both touched and saddened. He had never realised before this weekend how much this old woman meant to him, and how much he must mean to her in return. His lack of visits over the past few years must have really hurt her.

'You won't have to miss me any more, Gran,' was all he could think of to say. 'I'm home for good.'

'Home for good,' she repeated dazedly, as though still not daring to believe him. Her sigh was deep. 'I really do have to confess all now,' she said. 'Nothing else will do.'

'Well, they say confession is good for the soul,' Edward said as he wheeled himself over and patted his wife's knee. 'Isn't that right, love?'

Beverly lifted her tear-stained face. 'But only if you forgive me.'

'Of course I forgive you. You're my wife and I love you.'

'Oh, Edward. That's all I've ever wanted to hear.'

'And we will forgive you too, Gran,' Ben insisted. 'Because we all love you. Now, tell us what you did that you think was so bad.'

She sucked in a deep breath and squeezed her eyes tightly shut. Ben had a feeling he already knew what was coming. Gran always had been a devious old witch.

'I made it all up,' she blurted out. 'All that stuff I had them put in the newspaper. It was all lies. No one was bullying me or threatening me. There hadn't been any harassing phone calls. At least, not *before* that story was printed. I always had every intention of selling the farm to Amber, here. I knew I couldn't live there much longer and I knew I'd never get a better offer.'

She dragged in another deep breath and let it out

with a long, shuddering sigh. 'It was all a ploy to get you to come home, Ben. When you didn't come home at Christmas I became very depressed. Then, when I thought you were going to marry some girl in Sydney, I became quite desperate. I'd been holding on to the hope that you'd still end up with Amber. I'd seen the way you acted whenever you ran into her. I wasn't sure if she felt the same way about you till she came out to the farm that day to offer to buy it. But all she wanted to talk about when we had a cup of tea together was you.

'I decided then and there that if I could somehow bring you home and throw you two together, nature would take its course and I would never have to be lonely again. I knew you still had the local paper sent to you, but I reckoned that some nice little story about my selling my land to the Hollingsworths wouldn't bring you home. I needed to be in trouble. I needed a scandal!'

'Gran, you old scallywag!' Ben exclaimed.

'Oh, don't try to make it sound less than it was, Ben. I was very wrong to do what I did. It was a very selfish act. I can see that now. I didn't stop to think about Amber's father's reputation, or Amber's own feelings, or how the townspeople who'd thought they might find employment at the complex might be affected. I pretended to myself I was thinking of the big picture, that all would be well which ended well.

'But straight away things seemed to go wrong. You and Amber argued the moment you hit town. *Real* harassing calls started coming in as soon as you put the phone back on the hook. I can't tell you how shocked I was when that happened. I could hardly believe it.'

Ben recalled how she'd gone pale at the time. He'd thought it had been fear, but it had been shock.

'And then last night,' she said in strangled tones, swallowing convulsively as her eyes began to swim again. 'I know I didn't kill Rocky with my bare hands, but I'm still responsible. And I will have to live with that for the rest of my life. I just hope you can forgive me,' she finished tearily.

'Oh, Gran, of course we forgive you,' Ben said, hugging her. 'But you must forgive yourself too. You didn't mean any real harm. And you've suffered enough.'

'I don't deserve to be forgiven,' she sniffed against Ben's shoulder.

'You deserve more than I can ever give you, Gran. You took me in when no one else would. You loved me when no one else could. Everything I am today I owe to you.'

'Oh, Ben, what a sweet thing to say.' She dashed away her tears and set the most loving eyes upon him. Then she smiled over at Amber. 'He's turned out rather well, don't you think, dear?'

'Very well,' Amber agreed. 'Don't you think so, Dad?'

'I couldn't ask for a better son-in-law. I liked him

from the moment I met him. And he's just what you need.'

'Oh, really?' Amber asked archly. 'And what's that?'

'Someone to love you as much as I love *my* wife. Since we're in the business of confessions here, then I would like to add my own blame to this unfortunate situation. I can see now how much I have neglected you, my dear,' he told his stunned-looking wife. 'You have my promise that not a day will go by from this moment that I won't tell you how much I love you and care about you.'

'Oh, Edward.' Beverly was visibly moved.

Ben was moved as well. He was beginning to see where Amber got her strength of character from. Her father was quite a man to say that in front of others.

'Come, my dear,' Edward went on. 'I think we'd better go, and leave these lovebirds to tell Pearl all their plans. I will presume, however, that you won't want to wait too long for the wedding?' he asked, with a wry twinkle in his eye.

Ben looked over at Amber, who flushed furiously.

'Good,' Edward said, a satisfied smile curving his mouth as his wife wheeled him out of the room.

Gran beamed her approval at Ben, then took Amber's face in her wrinkled hands and kissed her on both cheeks. 'Oh, you lovely, lovely girl. How can I ever thank you?'

'Well, I can think of three ways,' Amber returned,

surprising Gran *and* Ben. What on earth was the minx up to?

'Firstly, you're to get yourself really strong and well, because tomorrow I'm going to show you this simply divine cottage which I know you'd just love to live in. I was going to live in it myself, but it's just not large enough to raise a big family in.

'Secondly, I will need you to help babysit once I do have a baby, because I'm afraid I can't be a full-time sit-at-home mother just yet. I have a shopping complex to build!

'And, thirdly, you're not to get offended when I don't call any of my daughters Pearl.'

A besotted, bewitched and bewildered Gran naturally agreed to everything.

In the car, when Ben finally had Amber on her own, he asked her about the cottage and she gave him the oddest look. 'I'll take you there right now and show it to you, if you like.' And she swiftly swung the car round in the opposite direction.

Ben frowned. 'Why do I get the feeling I'm in the dark about something here?'

She laughed. 'You won't be in the dark, darling. Not this time. The windows in the main bedroom are large and catch the sunshine.'

Ben felt his flesh leap. 'You're a wicked woman. But I love you all the same.'

Amber's breath caught. 'Do you know that's the first time you've actually said that?'

'Is it? Shall I say it again?'

She beamed across at him. 'Please do.'

'I love you, Amber Hollingsworth. Will you marry me?'

She gave him a startled look.

He shrugged. 'I haven't actually asked you, you know. So what do you say?'

'Er…'

'*Amber!*'

'Yes. I say yes!'

'I can see you're going to need a very firm hand. And often.'

'Yes, my love,' she said meekly, and Ben laughed.

He was still laughing when she pulled him into the cottage bedroom and started ripping off his clothes.

Eighteen months later, the *Sunrise Gazette* carried the following front page story:

SUNRISE'S AMBITIOUS NEW COMPLEX OPENS!

Last weekend, the long-awaited opening of Sunrise Point's new shopping and cinema complex went off very well, its ribbon being cut by the town's new Mayor, Edward Hollingsworth, who was helped by his lovely wife, Beverly. Looking on proudly was his daughter, Managing Director of Hollingsworths, Mrs Amber Sinclair. She was accompanied by her husband, local solicitor Ben Sinclair, who told the *Gazette* he was very proud of his wife and all she had accomplished for the town.

The only hiccup in the day's proceedings was when a greyhound galloped at speed through the car park and the centre, frightening a few people, before settling down sedately at the feet of Mrs Amber Sinclair.

The dog was quickly leashed and returned home to its owner, well-known local figure Mrs Pearl Sinclair, who was babysitting her great-grandson at the time. When asked for a comment about her speedy runaway, Mrs Sinclair said this was not the first time Gonzales had shown a drooling obsession for his favourite visitor and that she was not going to beat her head up against a brick wall. She was going to give the infernal animal to her grand-daughter-in-law and buy a cat!

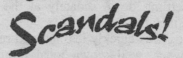

HARLEQUIN WOMEN
KNOW ROMANCE
WHEN THEY SEE IT.

And they'll see it on **ROMANCE CLASSICS**, the new 24-hour TV channel devoted to romantic movies and original programs like the special **Romantically Speaking—Harlequin™ Goes Prime Time.**

Romantically Speaking—Harlequin™ Goes Prime Time introduces you to many of your favorite romance authors in a program developed exclusively for Harlequin® readers.

Watch for **Romantically Speaking—Harlequin™ Goes Prime Time** beginning in the summer of 1997.

If you're not receiving ROMANCE CLASSICS, call your local cable operator or satellite provider and ask for it today!

Escape to the network of your dreams.

See Ingrid Bergman and Gregory Peck in *Spellbound* on Romance Classics.

Harlequin Romance®
and Harlequin Presents®

**bring you two great new miniseries
with one thing in common—MEN!
They're sexy, successful and available!**

You won't want to miss these exciting romances
by some of your favorite authors,
written from the male point of view.

Harlequin Romance® brings you

Starting in January 1998 with Rebecca Winters,
we'll be bringing you one **Bachelor Territory** book
every other month. Look for books by Val Daniels,
Emma Richmond, Lucy Gordon, Heather Allison
and Barbara McMahon.

Harlequin Presents® launches **MAN TALK**
in April 1998 with bestselling author Charlotte Lamb.
Watch for books by Alison Kelly, Sandra Field and
Emma Darcy in June, August and October 1998.

◆ HARLEQUIN®   *There are two sides to every story...
and now it's his turn!*

Coming Next Month

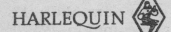

HARLEQUIN PRESENTS®

THE BEST HAS JUST GOTTEN BETTER!

#1935 LOVESTRUCK Charlotte Lamb
Nathalie's boss, Sam, was a little the worse for wear when he proposed to her at a party, so she decided to play along and pretend she believed he meant it. And soon she was really beginning to wish he *had*....

#1936 SCANDALOUS BRIDE Diana Hamilton
(Scandals!)
Nathan's whirlwind marriage was already heading for the rocks—he was sure his wife was having an affair with her boss! It seemed the only way to save the marriage was to learn the truth about his scandalous bride once and for all....

#1937 MISTRESS AND MOTHER Lynne Graham
Since separating on their wedding day, Molly maintained that nothing could persuade her to share her husband's bed.... Until Sholto agreed to settle her brother's debt—in return for the wedding night he never had!

#1938 THE LOVE-CHILD Kathryn Ross
(Nanny Wanted!)
When Cathy turned up at Pearce Tyrone's villa in the south of France, he assumed she was the nanny he'd been waiting for. But she knew it was only a matter of time before he found out that she wasn't all she seemed....

#1939 SECOND MARRIAGE Helen Brooks
(Husbands and Wives 2)
Claire would make the perfect bride—everyone said so. But Romano Bellini didn't want his life complicated by a second wife. Curious, then, that the subject of marriage just kept coming up!

#1940 THE VALENTINE AFFAIR! Mary Lyons
Alex had promised her newspaper a Valentine exclusive on Leo Hamilton. And after dogging Leo's all-too-attractive heels, she realized she wanted him as an exclusive, all right—exclusively hers!